AWAKEN

A NOVEL BY
TIMOTHY GEORGE

For Bedford Frederick (1949 – 1969).

ACKNOWLEDGEMENTS

I am extremely grateful to those whose contributions have enhanced this work. I want to thank my family and friends for their support and encouragement to make this idea into a reality.

I also want to acknowledge authors like Adam Hochschild for his book "King Leopold's Ghost" that brought the true story of what happened in the Belgium Congo to life. Ivan Van Sertima's ground breaking book, "They Came before Columbus," which includes research that chronicled African presence in Ancient America prior to Columbus' voyage. Mr. Sertima's thoughtful research for this book and others he has written have provided a much-needed reexamination of African history. There are many other authors that toiled at researching African history to whom I will be eternally grateful because their work allowed me to learn about the richness of African history and to appreciate how we are all connected.

Be extremely subtle, even to the point of formlessness. Be extremely mysterious, even to the point of soundlessness. Thereby you can be the director of the opponent's fate.

The Art of War, Sun Tzu.

CONTENTS

CHAPTER 1
FAMILY REUNION

The North Central Express always ran on time. The sleek commuter train was overflowing with people wanting to avoid driving in the snow in Chicago. The last person to board was Thomas Jet, he had to run two blocks to avoid missing the last train home. He settled into a seat near a window and started reading the paper. Sleep on the train came easy for Thomas. The bump, bump, bump rocked him fast to sleep. He never slept long, usually just a few minutes, and on this particular day, Thomas fell into a deep sleep on the way home. The train had reached the end of the line when his dream ended abruptly. Thomas jumped in his seat and looked around to see empty seats, except for the homeless man who was standing over him.

At first, Thomas thought he was about to be mugged, but relaxed when the elderly man told Thomas he had screamed in his sleep, so the man came over to check on him. He offered Thomas some of his beer, but Thomas refused, irritated that he had missed his stop.

The dream had seemed so real and life-like it had scared him. His shirt was soaking wet, but he was glad to see the smelly old man in his tattered jacket. The image of an ancient African woman lingered in his mind from his dream.

* * * * *

After the dream, Thomas reflected on his trip a month earlier, Thomas had started a different journey when he went on vacation to attend a family reunion in South Carolina. Being from Chicago, Thomas remembered the murder of Emmit Till and his ill-fated trip to Mississippi. Although the South has changed since the 50's, but those thoughts lingered in his mind. A pickup truck merged into the lane ahead of his car. In the back window, he could see the confederate flag and a gun rack. Thomas' apprehension grew as he drove away from the comfort of the bright lights of the cosmopolitan skyline of Atlanta. Of course, he had traveled to the South before, going to cities like Atlanta, New Orleans, and Memphis, but he had never ventured out from the city.

The trip required driving 160 miles to a village near Greenwood, South Carolina. The only way to get there was a three-hour drive. After an hour into his journey, Thomas found himself on a two-lane highway. Large oak trees lined the roadway as his car weaved around curvy back roads and through the occasional town. Most towns had one traffic light, which marked the business district with a feed store and a gas station. He kept a careful eye on his speedometer hoping to avoid a friendly sheriff eager to tag a Yankee passing through.

The bright orange, brown, and red leaves on the trees seemed to welcome the fall season with a tapestry of color. Thomas stopped several times to take pictures of the trees to document his pilgrimage to his father's family homestead. Finally, according to the handwritten directions his deceased father had left him, he arrived at the last town before he would get to his destination. This particular community had the distinction of having a flashing yellow traffic light, which indicated he only had five more miles to go. He turned left at the light. On either side of the road was a cotton field. It smelled of fresh plowed fields mixed in with manure. After a while, he became accustomed to the aroma and wondered what life in the rural South would be like. The countryside was beautiful, but the pace was too slow for Thomas.

As the sun went down, open fields turned into deep thick woods that hugged the narrow road. There were no streetlights or houses, just red clay hills and trees in sight. Thomas started to wonder if traveling to visit family he'd never met before was a good idea. He had been a toddler when his father moved away from Georgia, so Thomas was curious about why no one from his father's family had ever visited. He thought he would probably be the only stranger at the reunion, but he had promised his dad before he died that he would attend so he could meet the rest of the family.

After driving three hours, he arrived at the meetinghouse, which was tucked into a hill behind 100-year-old oak trees. The house, as his dad had told the story, was where freed slaves in the county used to meet after a long week of work. It belonged to the plantation overseer before the civil war.

Thomas' father's ancestors lived there during the South's reconstruction period. The house had a long history in his family. It had served as the church, a doctor's office and a dance hall for the young folks during segregation, and while Jim Crow remained the law in the Old South. His father told him the house was restored as a historical site when Lyndon Johnson became president. The family reunion had been held there every year in the fall ever since.

Thomas noticed cars in the parking lot. Out back behind the building, he saw smoke rising from a red brick barbecue pit. The aroma of ribs and smoked brisket made him hungry. He spotted men busy tending the fire and preparing supplies for the evening's festivities. Thomas walked up and introduced himself to a distinguished looking man sitting in a rocking chair near the entrance to the dining hall. The man stood up, extended his hand, and introduced himself as Dr. Oble. As he took Thomas' hand, he embraced him with a warm hug and said, "Welcome home, Jessie. Fufua!" Thomas was happy to be greeted warmly.

Thomas told the man it was good to meet him and began to explain that his name was not Jessie.

"My name is Thomas Jet. Are we related?"

"No," responded Dr. Oble. "I'm here with Otis Dinkins. I am from DC. Otis invited me to come visit South Carolina and get some good home cooking. Your father told me your name is Jessie." He looked at Thomas, as if he could not see him.

Dr. Oble had a gentle way about him. Thomas was puzzled by his response to his question. Thomas wondered if Dr. Oble might be senile. He started easing away from him but Dr. Oble pulled his arm, squeezing so hard he had to jerk back.

The old man asked Thomas, "Why have you wasted your time? Are you running from your destiny?"

"Are you talking to me?" responded Thomas.

"Yes. Aren't you Jessie from Chicago?" replied Dr. Oble.

"No. My name is Thomas," he reiterated while rubbing his arm. Thomas was surprised that the old man had such a strong grip. "My father used to call me Jessie, a nickname after my late uncle, but Jessie died when I was a child. My dad used to say I looked like his twin. How did you know that?"

"Your father told me," Dr. Oble responded.

"How did you meet my father?" asked Thomas.

"He spoke to me when I saw you walking up the hill," said the old man.

Thomas smiled and started laughing. "Okay, enough… you are playing a little game with me. How do you really know me?"

"No, no, I do not know your family. I only know what your father told me."

Before Thomas could ask more questions, a woman walked up. "So you've met our Dr. Oble." She explained that Dr. Oble was visiting from Ghana. She introduced herself as Aunt Betsy. "That's what everybody calls me, and now you've met your Aunt Betsy." Aunt Betsy was a large woman with large breasts that hung low. Her eyes were bright and alive, and she smiled as if she'd never met a stranger.

Aunt Betsy gave Thomas a big hug and pointed toward the bar where a man was holding a fish sandwich and a beer. She said, "That's my son Otis. He and Dr. Oble drove down from DC to visit me and eat some real food. After you get some home cooking you will feel right at home. Welcome home!" She called Otis over and told him to show Thomas around and introduce him to the rest of the family.

Thomas still did not understand how Dr. Oble could call him by his nickname and say he knew his father, but not his family. Thomas exchanged greetings and walked away with Otis. When he mentioned Dr. Oble in conversation with Otis and other family members, they all said "Yes, he has the gift". Apparently, Thomas was not the only one who'd had a unique encounter with him.

Otis introduced Thomas to his cousin Frankie. Frankie was Thomas' cousin from his grandmother's brother's side of the family. He said, "Dr. Oble is a psychic seer. According to Cousin Otis, he received his PhD from the university in Ghana."

"Is he a preacher or minister in Ghana?" questioned Thomas.

Frankie said, "He is more like a spiritual person."

"What is a seer?" asked Thomas.

"I'm not an expert or anything, but from what I understand it's sort of a like psychic but with an African twist," responded Frankie.

Thomas asked what Frankie thought of him. "He is kind of scary in the way he can say things. He seems to be a good gentle soul who is just different from what we are accustomed to here," said Frankie.

After getting more information on Dr. Oble, Thomas decided he would learn what else the old man knew about his family. Dr. Oble said, "Jessie, I'm glad you came back to talk to me. I sensed you needed to hear more about your father." Thomas was disturbed by his insistence on discussing his father.

"My father is deceased. I do not want to talk about him," declared Thomas.

Dr. Oble said, "Oh no, I am talking of your birth father from Africa from which your family's original seed was cast."

Thomas pointed his finger at Dr. Oble saying, "I am not from Africa. I'm from Chicago. My home is America. You got me confused with those back to Africa brothers. I am happy right here in the US of A."

"Your father will call you home when you are ready," whispered Dr. Oble.

"I don't understand why a university-trained PhD would speak in such double talk," responded Thomas.

Dr Oble smiled, "You're right. Your heart has to be open to your father's call to you, let me explain. I'm a spiritual elder for my tribal council in Ghana. Some call me a seer. The gift given to me at birth allows me to look into the souls of people to provide guidance. My father was a seer as his father was before him. I come from a family line of seven generations of seers. Years ago, your government's **Central Intelligence Agency (CIA)** had a program for 'remote viewing.' It is a documented fact that certain people have a gift and can see things. The program was used to gather information for criminal investigations and cold war intelligence purposes. If you do not believe me, Google remote viewing."

Thomas got agitated. "I'm not interested in the CIA, remote viewing or any other African Voodoo."

At this point, Thomas changed the subject, then exchanged business cards with the doctor and returned to the festivities of the family reunion.

* * * * *

Two weeks later, back in Chicago, Dr. Oble's card fell out of Thomas' pants pocket as he was putting clothes in the car to take to the cleaners. Later that evening, Thomas studied the card and found where he had written "remote viewing" on the back. He had started this habit a while ago when he met new people. He would write key words to remind him of the person or the topic of conversation. However, Dr. Oble was not hard to remember.

With his favorite scotch and last Cuban cigar in hand, Thomas sat on his patio with his laptop and typed "remote viewer" into Google. To his surprise, there were many links on the topic although none focused on African viewers or Dr. Oble. Several described what the old man had told Thomas at the family reunion. "This is going to require a little more scotch," Thomas mumbled. Fortunately, he had just opened the bottle. Thomas sipped and read for most of the evening and learned more than he ever wanted to know about the topic. The drink helped him consider the possibility that Dr. Oble really was who he said he was.

The next morning, while having his coffee, Thomas remembered what the seer told him concerning his birth father. This gave him an eerie feeling. Thomas did not believe in tarot cards, reading tealeaves or any other paranormal mumbo jumbo. With a PhD in psychology, Dr. Oble did not fit the profile of kooks who gave readings for twenty dollars on the street corner. He seemed like a credible person. Thomas put the business card away and went to work.

Thomas worked as an investment banker for commercial real estate developments. His workday was hectic. His head was still a little foggy from the cocktails he'd consumed the night before. The phones were ringing off the hook and most of the day was spent responding to emails and attending hour-long conference calls. At the end of the day, as Thomas started loading his brief case and preparing for the commute home, he got a call from a friend and client in Mclean, Virginia—Jack Regis.

"Thomas, I'm in a bind. I need your help. The bank is threatening to pull their funding commitment if I don't get the final details worked out with the contractors. I'm desperate I could lose the firm if this deal goes bad."

"Slow down, I've got too much work to do here. I cannot drop everything to come to Virginia," responded Thomas.

Jack pleaded, "It will only take a day or two. I need your help."

"Okay, I will move around a few things here and will be there on Friday," responded Thomas.

Jack and Thomas served in the army together twenty years ago in the infantry. Jack talked Thomas into attending officer's training together to make a career in army intelligence. Thomas retired early as a captain, but Jack stayed in. They kept in touch. Jack worked in military intelligence and for the US State Department before he retired to take over his dad's real-estate development business. They had done several real estate deals together, and Jack knew if the chips were down, he could count on his friend to pull his bacon out of the fire.

Unfortunately, the trip required Thomas to stay over the weekend. In the taxi on the way to the airport, as Thomas was shuffling through his briefcase, he found Dr. Oble's business card stuffed in his iPod case. This card just seemed to keep turning up. He thought since he would be in the DC area anyway, maybe he should give Dr. Oble a call to check if he would be in town.

When Thomas called him, Dr. Oble responded, "Hello, Jessie, I was expecting your call. Yes, I will be available. I can meet you on Saturday at 2:30 at the Marriott in Alexandria."

Thomas was more emphatic this time. "My name is Thomas, not Jessie. Let us get this straight for the last time. Do you always hold one-way conversations? I did not even get in a 'hello' before you agreed to meet me."

"Okay, Thomas," Dr. Oble said with compassion in his voice. "I'll try to do better with your name. I am sorry about the speed-read conversation. My friends have gotten used to me, and they say I save them minutes on their mobile phone bills. Please do not let my gift put you off. I mean no harm. I would like to bring someone with me on Saturday. After we met at your family reunion, I knew you needed to meet Erd. Her name is Miss Oshalo Seehwo Erd from Zimbabwe, but I call her Erd. You will like her. She is a seer with great skill."

Thomas told him the time and place were okay and ended the call. He felt no need to say much more since Dr. Oble had already hung up the phone.

* * * * *

High winds and heavy rains tossed the small regional jet around like a toy. Thomas gripped the armrest and dug his fingernails into the leather cover. The plane dropped ten thousand feet in less than a minute, causing several passengers to become sick as the pilot circled the hills of Virginia while waiting for permission to land. His palms were sweating, thinking the plane was going to crash. Thomas' heart pounded as he watched lighting strike near the wing outside his window. He closed the window shade hoping this would lower his anxiety, but it did not help. Thoughts of things he left undone rushed through his mind. He thought about the meeting with the mysterious Dr. Oble as part of his list of things yet to be completed. Thomas' stomach calmed when the pilot announced the plane was preparing for landing. When the plane landed the wheels made a loud pop, then the plane began to shake violently until it came to a stop short of the gate.

Thomas asked the flight attendant, "What happened?" She looked at him but said nothing, and then the pilot's voice came over the loud speaker. "A tire on the landing gear blew out. All passengers will deplane on the tarmac."

Thomas gathered his luggage and muttered a prayer in thanks for a safe arrival, thinking he could handle anything else that happened after this flight from hell. He hoped the tormented flight was not an omen about this trip. He arrived at the hotel at 2:00 in the morning, too late for room service. However, thanks to Mid-Chicago Air he had already lost his appetite. He smiled, thinking he should find another way home. Maybe, take the train. He ate the chocolate left on the pillow by his considerate hotel host and slipped into a deep sleep.

His meeting with Jack the next day went as well as could be expected. They met for eight punishing hours with bankers and contractors. There was no break for lunch, as Jack had arranged for tuna sandwiches and all the coffee they could drink. Finally, the parties agreed to leave some money on the table to complete the deal. Thomas even got his arm twisted for part of his fee. Jack and Thomas had done many deals together. Jack would make it up on the next one. Thomas had considered giving up the whole fee for some real food and release from the conference room. Everyone was close to a breaking point, even Jack, who was showing the fatigue from two months of trying to get this transaction done. After signing the documents, Jack insisted Thomas join him for a steak dinner, a celebratory drink and a cigar. Jack was relieved to be finished.

"Why aren't you leaving in the morning? I'll spring for a first class ticket to get you home by Saturday night," Jack stated with renewed confidence.

"Thanks Jack, I thought we would be meeting through the weekend and made plans to meet a friend tomorrow afternoon. I'd like to ask you a favor, if it will not be breaking any security protocols," Thomas said as he packed papers into his briefcase.

Jack coughed into his drink. "Thomas, this sounds serious."

"Not really. I need a little information. Could you check out someone for me? I met this guy named Dr. Oble a few weeks ago, and I'd like some background information on him before I meet him tomorrow," replied Thomas.

Jack was puzzled. "I thought you said you were meeting a friend. This doesn't sound like a friendly meeting to me, with background checks and all."

"Well, I met him a short while ago. He has an unusual story. I would just like confirmation that all the dots connect, based on some of the things he told me," responded Thomas.

"Are you planning to do a deal with him? Is this something I would be interested in? I owe you one," Jack grinned.

"No," Thomas said. "He is an acquaintance whom I met at a family reunion. I just want a little more information about him."

"Okay, Thomas, I'll have the data for you in the morning. Give me what you have on him," Jack responded as he pulled out his PDA.

"He is a PhD from the University of Ghana working on a research project at Howard University. That's everything. Oh, here is his business card," Thomas answered.

Jack spoke hurriedly as he put the data into his Blackberry. "No problem. I will get you a profile from one of my friends at the State Department. There will be an envelope under your door in the morning. Now let's find that steak and a couple of glasses of twenty-five-year-old single malt. I may be able to finagle a few Cuban cigars after dinner."

Thomas patted Jack on the back and smiled. "Now you're talking. I'm ready."

After dinner, Jack took Thomas to his favorite cigar bar. They sampled scotch until they settled into the best of the house. After the third drink and halfway through his cigar, Thomas comfortably settled back in a brown leather chair. He said, "Jack, are you familiar with something called remote viewing?"

"Thomas, after what you did for me today I will tell everything I know. It is not much. I never worked with the program, but I know a little. They use parapsychology for intelligence. The CIA and the army had an operation like that during the Cold War. The Russians had a program, too. The rumor mill is full of stories of how the CIA program used telepathic mind travel to spy undetected. At the time, it was believed this technique could be used worldwide. It is real. The key is the psychic gift level of the individuals in the program. From what I've heard, the best candidates for the program would not agree to participate. Therefore, the official word is the program never became operational beyond the experimental phase. If you need more information, let me know. I warn you my friend, do not poke around on your own. The true status of the project is not known," said Jack.

After delivering his words of wisdom and caution, Jack paid the check and left Thomas at the bar. Thomas had a few more drinks and finished his cigar while thinking about Dr. Oble, who was beginning to sound like the real deal. Thomas pushed his uncertain thoughts aside, preferring to think about it when he reviewed the data Jack would pull together. He returned to his hotel. The sheets were turned back and ready for him to pass out. He bypassed the chocolate and fell fast asleep.

Thomas woke himself up with a loud snore. He looked around the room to check the alarm clock, which showed 7:00. He went to the bathroom and found an envelope on the floor. At first he thought it was the hotel bill but remembered his check out was not until Sunday. *This must be from Jack,* he thought.

Jack's military training had not stopped when he retired. He was always punctual and followed up like clockwork. Thomas opened the envelope. Inside was a three-page dossier on Dr. Oble. No letterhead on the pages or address on the documents, the source was not traceable. Jack was thorough. Thomas had a headache from too much scotch, food, and cigars, so he put the envelope in his jacket pocket and went back to bed.

Later, Thomas was waiting in the hotel lobby bar. He sat where he could spot Dr. Oble and his friend Miss Erd when they arrived. The old man was on time but without Miss Erd. Thomas waved and the good doctor came to greet him. He gave Thomas a warm embrace, with a hug as if he were a family member with strong ties. It seemed genuine. He again apologized about the phone conversation they had a few days earlier. He explained his gift was sometimes hard to contain, and he forgot to let the discussion unwind, instead of simply responding to the thoughts of the other party.

He said, "In my defense, my eighty-eight years are showing more than I would like to admit." This was one of the most shocking statements he'd made to Thomas during their brief acquaintance. Thomas told him he thought he could not be more than sixty years old. He could not have missed guessing the man's age by almost thirty years.

Dr. Oble said, "Yes, longevity is a positive side effect of this gift. I think I told you that I am the seventh generation. My father lived until he was one-hundred-fifteen and his father before him lived to the age of one-hundred-twenty. Our family has been responsible for this gift for over seven hundred years. Time moves slowly through our family and we pass history from generation to generation."

"Are you telling me you are holding hundreds of years of history in your mind?" Thomas quietly asked as he tried not to look perplexed.

Dr. Oble responded, "No, it is not easy to say how much information I have. It is not indexed by calendar days or time periods. To be honest, I do not know what data I do retain. My father transferred his oral history to me, as his father did to him and so on. Technically, I retain the collective histories of seven generations. Unfortunately, I do not have the key to access the information. This is why I came to the States to study. I came to do take advanced studies in psychology at Howard University in order to determine if there is another way to access my memory. Miss Erd is the other reason I came to DC.

She has a tremendous clairvoyant gift. I hope to learn from her. This is why I wanted her to meet you."

Again Thomas asked, "Why me? I can't remember what happened last week without my Blackberry. I cannot read your mind or anyone else's for that matter. I think you are confused about me."

"Please do not get upset. I'm not sure, but I think you also have the gift," responded Dr. Oble.

Thomas' tone quickly turned argumentative. "No way, I'm not like you. I have a successful career, a house, mortgage, and a dog. I do not see dead people."

Dr. Oble responded, "I know this is all strange to you, and it's possible I'm wrong. For some folks, the gift is suppressed, and it does not surface until a catalyst sparks the emergence."

Thomas said, "It does not sound like a gift to me. It sounds more like a curse. I do not want any part of this murky psycho world."

Dr. Oble studied Thomas' face, seeing that his reaction was of fear and disbelief. Dr. Oble explained, "It is not that simple. It is more complex. I cannot sit here and reel off seven hundred years of memories about people, events and places at one sitting. This would overwhelm anyone, even me, with my modest gift."

"Why me?" Thomas asked again. "You said when you met me at the reunion that you heard my African birth father speak. What did you mean by that? Did you have a connection with anyone else at the family reunion?"

Dr. Oble said, "No, you are the only one. Of course, I knew you would be there and here today. I had hoped Miss Erd would be here by now, but she had a conflict. She will be late. She could help me explain, but I will try. The information passed to me by my father, and my father's father is in the form of images and oral histories. The history is recalled if I am queried for data. A word, place or visual recognition in some instances can spark a response. In most cases, I need to put myself into a meditative state to access information that I possess. You have to remember, computers are a relatively new invention in the last sixty years or so. My data is from the past seven hundred years. When I saw your face, it triggered an automatic response, and I told you what I heard and what the images presented to me."

Thomas stared at him, puzzled. "I don't understand!"

Dr. Oble explained, "Somewhere in my memory is your father's, father's, father who started your family line in Africa. Your life here, as in Africa, is recorded and connected. What does this mean? I do not know. I have only been in this country for six months and the trip to South Carolina was my first trip outside of DC."

Thomas asked, "Can you tell me more about my African father?"

He responded, "No, I can only see his face and yours. I hear your birth father calling you Jessie, but no more than that."

Thomas questioned him again. "I don't understand why you cannot tell me more."

"Your African father may have been part of a royal family or an extended family," Dr. Oble explained, "If he recorded a message for you, he would have been at least in the royal court. Erd is more gifted than I. She can answer your questions more clearly."

Dr. Oble's phone rang. It was a call from his friend Erd. "She will not meet us," he mumbled, sounding clearly disappointed. He told Thomas of his burden, explaining that the responsibility of holding the secrets of strangers in his memory was enormous. He explained that he'd obtained a master's degree and doctorate in psychology. Hypnotic regression into past lives was his specialty. He hoped this study would enable him to understand how to tap into the histories passed to him.

Typically, he explained, the village shaman possessed the keys. The shaman would start by chanting a series of incantations that put him into a trance. At this point, he would respond to key phrases to unlock memories and the data kept in his trust. These phrases were kept secret. Unfortunately, Africa lost millions of its people over the last five hundred years because of slavery and colonization. Dr. Oble's village shaman was killed in 1953.

He said, "Therefore, I do not have access to the keys to the memories I hold. I can only unlock these memories now by chance, like when I met you at the family reunion. This has happened many times in

Africa but my revelations are fragments and difficult to piece together."

Thomas was captivated by this story. It sounded like a plot from a B movie. As he sat there listening to Dr. Oble explain his situation and his search for answers, Thomas thought the story was amazing. If he had not seen and heard this for himself, he would not believe it. Thomas and Dr. Oble discussed what he planned to do to obtain the keys to his memory. He was uncertain and hoped Miss Erd could help him gain access. However, the work had been slow and tedious. He explained Miss Erd encouraged him to go with Otis to the family reunion. She said he would find a fellow traveler in South Carolina who would help him with his journey to find the keys he needed.

"You are connected to me, but I am not sure how," continued Dr. Oble. "That's why I am disappointed she cannot come today."

"I cannot help you. I wish I could but I do not know anything," said Thomas.

Continuing the visit, Thomas decided to change the topic. They talked about politics, soccer, and Dr. Oble's village near Kumasi, in Ghana. As Dr. Oble prepared to leave, he reached inside his jacket pocket and handed Thomas a gold medallion with a symbol on both sides.

Dr. Oble said, "At home in Ghana, there is an old system of symbols called Adinkra. A mythical bird that flies forward with his head turned backward symbolizes Sankofa, which means "return to your roots." This reflects the Akan belief that there is wisdom in learning from the past. Please accept this token as a gift from me."

He embraced Thomas as his brother and quickly departed from the café before Thomas could say anything. Intrigued by the mysterious Dr. Oble, Thomas put the item in his pocket.

The next morning Thomas boarded his plane back to Chicago. He crossed his fingers when the flight attendant announced that the door was closed, and they were ready for takeoff.

CHAPTER 2
UNCLE JESSIE

Uncle Jessie and Mr. Jet moved to Chicago shortly after Thomas' birth. They never returned to Georgia to visit anyone, and lost touch with any family they had in the South. Jessie passed away when Thomas turned seven years old. He had lived with Thomas and his father for as long as Thomas could remember. Thomas' mother died during childbirth. Only her picture remained as a memory of her presence and his father did not talk about her. Thomas never asked many questions.

Thomas' play mother whom he called Aunt Maggie was always around. She spent holidays and special occasions with him and his father even stood by at his baptism and applauded his graduation day. For all practical purposes, Maggie was Thomas's mother. Though she did not live with them, she had been a big part of his family. Mr. Jet, Uncle Jessie and Aunt Maggie were Thomas' only family. After Jessie died, Thomas' father started calling his son Jessie as sort of a nickname, which stuck until Thomas entered high school. No one had called Thomas by the name Jessie until he met Dr. Oble at the family reunion.

The memory of being fat in high school kept Thomas in the gym. His muscles bulged through his shirts. He wore tailored suits that accentuated his finely tuned physique and six foot frame. Hearing Dr. Oble call him Jessie brought memories of his journey to manhood racing through his mind.

Thomas was young when Uncle Jessie died, so he did not remember much about him, except that he used to read bedtime stories to him before he went to sleep. He recalled that Jessie had a great imagination because he told most of the stories from memory. Thomas believed Jessie made them up because his descriptions of colorful characters from faraway places would continue for hours. Often Thomas fell asleep, and woke up to find Jessie still telling his stories. Even during daylight old uncle Jessie would be talking to Thomas while he slept. He'd hum, sing a tune and chant. Thomas thought Jessie was lonely, and that's why he liked telling tales. Thinking back, Thomas realized he never remembered any of the details of stories the next day, though occasionally, his imagination would create images of some of the characters in his stories. Jessie did not have much formal schooling. He spoke broken English and always encouraged Thomas to do his lessons, learn, and remember.

Thomas called his Aunt Maggie after he returned from DC. He had questions concerning Uncle Jessie. Happy to hear from him, she asked about the business and his trip to DC. When he asked about Uncle Jessie, she got quiet and the phone went silent.

"Why are you asking about Jessie? His bones have turned to dust. You should be thinking of your future, finding a good wife and making some babies," responded Maggie.

Thomas said, "I need to learn more about him. I met someone at the family reunion who called me Jessie. He claims he recognized Jessie by looking at me. It is a long story I do not want to go into. Tell me more about him."

She started crying and did not speak for a few minutes, then Maggie said, "Your father should be here to talk to you about Jessie. I told him many times he needed to tell you, but he was stubborn like a mule. He wouldn't budge. He said you did not need to know anything, and everything would be just fine."

Thomas pleaded with Aunt Maggie. "You're the only mother, I've ever had. I do not care what it is. Nothing will change me. I just need questions answered about him. It seems there is some mystery around him."

She calmed herself down and said, "We should meet somewhere to talk. This is not a conversation for the telephone. Can you come over on Sunday afternoon for supper and apple cobbler? I will tell you everything. Son, you can count on me for anything." Thomas accepted her invitation for dinner, which was always a treat, but he wondered what caused such a strange reaction in Aunt Maggie.

On Sunday, Thomas pulled into the driveway at Aunt Maggie's. The yard was green, manicured, with roses and lilies lining the pathway to the front door. Her home was a brownstone located in the city near Lakeshore Drive. He did not think she ever worked, but she lived well. As a child, Thomas used to spend the weekends at her house and played with the kids who lived next door.

This visit was different from any Thomas had made before. He smelled fried chicken and apple cobbler as he rang the doorbell. The aroma helped him forget why he had come. Thomas gave Aunt Maggie a big hug and went straight to the kitchen. He grabbed a chicken wing and wolfed it down before she found him in the study. She had never liked for him to sample food before dinner when he was a kid, and this had not changed over all these years. She would slap his hand if she saw him reach for a taste of the meal she prepared. Today was no different.

After dinner, Maggie took Thomas outside to sit in the gazebo under the honey suckle vines that grew up the poles and over the top. The yard resembled a park, with a fountain and flowers surrounded by plants she brought from Georgia. It reminded her of her mother's place. She called it her sanctuary. The fact that she wanted to talk there meant whatever she needed to tell him must be important.

Maggie sat beside Thomas, patted his hand, and said, "Son, you are a grown man. I watched you grow with your father. I am proud of you. He loved you dearly, and you were the most important person in the world to him."

"I cannot imagine growing up with anyone other than you and dad in my life. What about Uncle Jessie?" asked Thomas.

She pulled a tissue out of her pocket, took a deep breath. She said, "I am going to tell you about Jessie. He was from Georgia, like your father and me. He was older than your dad. I left Georgia five years before your father and Jessie moved to Chicago. Your father contacted me right before they left town to move north. He asked me if I would help him, Jessie, and you find a place to live in the city. Your father told me you were his son. Your mother had died in childbirth, and Jessie was your mother's brother. Your parents had not married. After y'all settled in, we had your birth certificate changed to add your father's last name. A few years later, your father confided in me that Jessie was really your father. He said Jessie was in some trouble with the government, and he was on the run. When you were born your mother died, and Jessie asked your father to help him with you. After Jessie died, we thought there was no need to tell you about him being your father. We did not know if the government was still looking for Jessie or whether his trouble would become your trouble." Maggie started crying uncontrollably until Thomas finally got her to calm down.

Thomas asked Maggie, "Why did dad take on such responsibility for Jessie?"

She said, "Your father would not discuss it. He said this is men's business. You do not talk about some things. You know your father. He had a stubborn streak a mile wide, so I stopped asking. We all settled in as an extended family and raised you as our own. Son, leave the dead with the dead. I pray you leave Dr.Oble alone. Go find yourself a good wife and bring me some grandchildren."

Thomas hugged Maggie. She fixed him a plate of dinner to take with him and surprised him with a sweet potato pie. Half the pie made it to his house. The rest he ate in the car on the way. Aunt Maggie's pie was a delicacy he could not resist.

Later that night he pulled out his family album and examined the pictures of his father, Uncle Jessie and Aunt Maggie. The images took on a new meaning to him as he looked into their eyes and wondered why his father had helped Jessie. Thomas looked into the mirror and could see his smooth brown complexion and high cheekbones were more like Uncle Jessie's than his father's. He stood there for a few minutes, as if he had discovered someone new looking back at him. Thomas thought, "Who is Uncle Jessie? Who am I?"

When Thomas fell asleep on the train coming home from work a month later, he dreamed about Uncle Jessie and an African woman. The woman appeared ancient, not human, but more spirit-like with a weathered body and a weary expression on her face, which could be hundreds or thousands of years old. Her face, narrow and thin, looked full of sorrow. She had long arms and dark and piercing eyes. She sat silently in a chair that resembled a throne. She would simply motion with her hands and point with her thin fingers. Jessie and Thomas were sitting in a crowd before her when she reached out to touch Jessie. When she touched Thomas, he jumped and woke up on the train. Every time he thought about that dream, he got a chill.

CHAPTER 3
FRESH START

Two months had passed since Aunt Maggie told Thomas the truth about Uncle Jessie before he decided to take her advice and move forward. He got busy at work, added several clients, and brought on additional staff to give him time to work on his personal life. He started dating again and to his surprise, very soon a woman was working her way into his crowded space. Since his divorce, Thomas had dismissed all thoughts of looking for a long-term relationship and usually ended most of his relationships after the third date. However, Nicolette had staying power.

Her mother was Ethiopian and her father was Spanish. She moved to Chicago to go to the University of Chicago and decided to stay. Nicolette's biggest complaint about Americans was that they had no sense of history. She believed Europeans had overcome more adversity than Americans. She was intelligent, funny, and outgoing. Thomas probably noticed her body first and then her other qualities opened his eyes to her potential as a longer-term interest. He could not do better than that, besides she was not looking for marriage and Thomas was fine with that.

Thomas felt like he had the wind to his back and moved full speed ahead. Literally, this was true because Nicolette's hobby was sailing. Thomas picked up the bug too. They had been out on Lake Michigan every weekend since they met. Thomas gained his confidence with the boat and even got Aunt Maggie out on the water. Of course, she had to put on two life preservers and held on the rail the entire time. Thomas thought Aunt Maggie was hoping Nicolette would be the one to give her some grand babies.

* * * * *

Thomas was sitting on the deck one afternoon daydreaming and watching the sunset while Nicolette was busy cutting the sails with Aunt Maggie, who was gingerly holding the tiller. When his mobile phone rang, he started to turn it off until he noticed Jack's number. He picked up the phone and said, "Hey Jack."

"Don't say a word. Call me at Smokey's tonight at 8:00. Use a payphone."

Thomas hung up and went over to help Nicolette and Aunt Maggie bring the boat into the marina. Nicolette took Aunt Maggie home while Thomas finished tying up and stowing the gear.

After Thomas purchased a phone card, he called Smokey's precisely at 8:00. Jack answered the phone and asked, "Are you alone, on a pay phone?"

"Yes. I followed your instructions to the tee."

Jack responded, "Thomas, sorry about the secrecy but we've got a problem. I had my phones checked last week and a security firm discovered listening devices on the home and office phones. Three weeks ago, my friend Herb Jenkins at the State Department died in a one-car accident. At first, I thought it was an accident until I reviewed the police report. I suspected foul play. Shortly thereafter, someone broke into my office but nothing was stolen. Now the phones are bugged. I think your friend Dr. Oble is linked to these events."

"Jack, there must be another explanation. Dr. Oble is a little strange but he is not a spy or secret agent. I cannot believe this," responded Thomas.

Jack waited a few minutes and in a low voice said, "Thomas, I know about these things. All the arrows are pointing to him. Did you read the dossier I gave you on him?"

Thomas responded hesitantly, "Well. I browsed through the first page and confirmed everything he told me, but I did not read further. I was hung over and simply scanned the document. I still have it in my office."

Jack said, whispering, "You need to read the entire document. Dr. Oble has no history beyond his attendance at a college in Ghana. He is an orphan with no family. He has no visible means of support other than a government research grant. He is a ghost. If he disappeared today, you would not be able to locate him. His passport is the world map. Dr. Oble traveled extensively in Africa, Europe, the Caribbean, and South America. His credentials carry a diplomatic status. This is unusual for a college professor. I don't want to scare you, but I'm concerned."

Thomas digested everything Jack had to say and thought about his response carefully. "If what you suspect is true I need to contact him to get some answers. This situation may not go away on its own. Whoever broke into your office will find me if they got to you and your friend Herb. Dr. Oble approached me concerning Uncle Jessie when we first met. I later learned Uncle Jessie is really my father. He had a crazy story about being a seer or remote viewer and his capacity for storing oral histories in his memory. He also said he needed a series of keys to unlock the meaning of the memories. This is where he hoped I would help him. Nevertheless, up until now I thought he was somewhat crazy. Since then, I've learned more about my real father and his past. Some of the puzzle pieces are falling into place. I still do not understand why someone would be killed for doing a background check."

"Thomas, you should tread carefully," said Jack. "I agree with you. You need to find out more about him and his connection to you. I am going to do some checking on him and your father with a friend at the CIA to determine if the red flags on them are from our side. Do not call me. I will contact you. Do not talk to anyone about this, not even Aunt Maggie. Find the briefing paper. Read and burn it. I will be back in touch in a few days. Good luck." The phone went dead.

The sound of the dial tone in Thomas's ear put him in a daze. He stood in the phone booth looking at the horizon on Lake Michigan. His mind was a million miles away. A man approached from behind. Thomas jumped and threw the phone against the wall.

The man said, "Mister are you okay? Are you finished with the phone?" Thomas motioned yes and walked away slowly, stopping occasionally to determine if he was being followed.

At his office, Thomas found the dossier on Dr. Oble tucked in the back of his desk drawer. He read the document carefully and confirmed what Jack said about Oble's missing past. He went to the garage and burned the document in the trash receptor as instructed. On the way home he thought, *What have I gotten myself into? Who is Dr. Oble? What does he want from me? Who am I?*

Thomas stopped by a discount store and purchased several disposable mobile phones to use for contacting Jack and for calling Dr. Oble to set up a meeting. He decided to take two-weeks off from work to avoid any suspicion from his staff about this situation. This vacation would also give him time to develop a plan.

Thomas dialed Dr. Oble's number. He answered. "Jessie, your journey is just beginning."

"Who are you? I need some answers and I need them now!" shouted Thomas.

Dr. Oble said, "Son…. You are upset. I cannot help you. The direction of your life was set generations before your birth. You have to find those answers. However, things have changed greatly since we met in Virginia. This phone is not safe. I can meet with you in person in two days. Go to the Baltimore InterHarbor Hotel and be in the lounge at 7:00." The phone went silent.

* * * * *

Travel to Baltimore would have to be by car because airplane and rental cars left paper trails. Thomas would have to use cash for gas and hotels. Thomas decided to drive to Cleveland and borrow his ex-college roommate's vehicle for the rest of the trip. He had watched enough spy movies to know how to cover some of his tracks. However, until he determined what he was up against, he would tell no one where he went or why. Thomas shaved his head to alter his appearance and changed his attire. Before his meeting with Dr. Oble, he needed to research Uncle Jessie and find out as much about him as possible. His father had stored some old boxes in the attic with family photos and papers. Thomas found only two pictures of Jessie. One from when they lived in Georgia and the other taken in Chicago. Jessie's bible recorded his birth date as 1878. This would have made him one hundred and five years old at his death. Back then, Thomas thought Jessie was in his seventies. He never celebrated birthdays or talked about his age.

Thomas went online to access the county courthouse records in Georgia to research his father and his family. The courthouse burned down fifty years ago and no other records were found. According to his bible, Jessie was married in Georgia but this was eighty years ago. Who is my mother, Thomas thought? The picture Thomas had only contained a first name but no last name. June was her name … if this is really his mother. His birth certificate only had June F for his mother. No last name. Thomas was born at home, so there were no hospital birth records. Aunt Maggie and his father had fixed up Thomas's birth certificate when they moved to Chicago. There was no paper trail.

Thomas thought aloud, "I have no past. My father is not my father, and my mother is unknown. Is she really dead? Who am I?"

In desperation, Thomas telephoned Aunt Betsy in South Carolina to determine if she had any information on Jessie. Aunt Betsy answered the phone, "Hello baby. I remember you. You are the skinny boy from Chicago. You are the Jet boy from Grandma Jenny's side of the family."

Thomas said, "Yes, my father was James Jet, from Georgia. Do you remember anything about Uncle Jessie Mende Richmond? He passed away thirty-five years ago, and I'm trying to pull together a family tree."

Aunt Betsy said to hold the phone. She came back, sounding out of breath, and said, "Did you say Jessie Mende from Georgia?"

Thomas said, "Yes."

She said, "Boy you're not related to him. I remember grandma talking about Jessie and the trouble up in Georgia. Jessie is not part of our family. His people are from South Carolina from a Geechee clan. I never met his people, but he talked like the Geechee. You know that African pig English. Grandma Jenny always tells the story about the gray suits that came looking for him. They went from farm to farm. They even had a picture of him. Yes son, Jessie was trouble. When the gray suits are looking for you…you run. That's federal trouble. Our kin kept to ourselves and stayed away from troublemakers like Jessie. Boy don't worry 'bout him. Leave the dead to the dead."

Thomas asked, "Aunt Betsy, how did Jessie get in trouble with the federal government?"

Betsy said, "Son back then you didn't need to do anything to get in trouble. Sometimes you just looked the wrong way, and they came after you. However, in Jessie's case, he made a group of white folks mad because he kept talking about his visions about Africa, Marcus Garvey and black power stuff. During the civil rights struggle in the South, that was trouble. They called you a communist if you got involved with all that marching and protest stuff. Even Martin Luther King was called a communist. Boy, I don't know what he did. The gray suits showed up, and he disappeared. Leave the dead with the dead. You come back next year for the reunion. We will fatten you up and put some meat on those bones. Just remember when you come here you're coming home."

Thomas said, "Thanks Aunt Betsy, I will try to make it next year."

She said, "Bless you son. Take care."

How did Thomas go from being an American to a Geechee in less than three months? What was a Geechee anyway? It sounded like a bird or something. Aunt Betsy had said that Uncle Jessie was a Geechee, but Thomas had no time for more research. He needed to get on the road to Cleveland.

Thomas thought, *What should I tell Nicolette and Aunt Maggie?* He knew that he would put them in danger if they found out the truth. *A business trip to Cleveland and a fraternity reunion in Nashville sounds about right*, he decided and dialed Nicolette's number and told her what he thought she would believe.

By the time Thomas finally cleared the rush-hour traffic and got on the road to Cleveland, he realized he had forgotten how much he enjoyed road trips. City driving took the joy out of owning his car. Thomas remembered when he bought the car, he'd found it on the street for sale by owner. He passed by it for weeks before finally deciding to stop and look. The car was an older model 500 SL Mercedes, gray with black interior and low profile tires. He'd looked through the window to see that the seats and carpet were in good condition. His dad would never have approved of this car. Mr. Jet always used to say, do not drive a car that costs more than a house. He would often complain of seeing black folks driving expensive cars while living in apartments. He was conservative and always drove cars ten years old or older. His father never bought foreign cars. He would say, "Son never buy foreign cars. They don't hire black folks. If they make the car in Detroit, a black person had a job." He was a Ford man who always drove a Ford. Thomas had respected his wishes and drove Fords, too, until now.

When his dad passed away his life insurance left Thomas some extra money after all the expenses were paid. The money was just sitting in the bank, and he kept passing by the car. When he called the number on the windshield, he spoke to the owner, who was an elderly woman who gave him all the information on the car. The car belonged to her husband who had recently passed away. She wanted to sell the car because it reminded her of him. The price was right and Thomas' father would have been happy that his son did not pay a new house price for the car. However, Thomas knew his father probably would not forgive him for buying foreign, but he bought the car and put custom plates on it. The name on his plates was Ford. Go figure. Ford and Thomas were headed to Cleveland.

Thomas let the convertible top down and drove without a thought in his head other than how much he liked his car. Thomas hated thinking of leaving his car with Frank, but this was the only way. If people were really, tracking him, they would have his plate number and car description. The Mercedes would stick out like a sore thumb. Frank had a minivan and would gladly trade the minivan for the Mercedes for a week.

Frank and Thomas were roommates in college. They pledged the same fraternity and graduated on time. The getting out on time part was amazing because they did their share of partying. Living in a frat house was not always conducive to scholarly pursuits. Frank was from Louisiana, and he loved cooking up some Creole dishes. Jambalaya, gumbo, crawfish, and fried oyster poor boys were the meals Frank contributed to the diet of starving college students.

Frank was the angry black man of the fraternity. He majored in Afro-American studies. He would lecture the brothers, whenever they would listen about the movement, apartheid or anything concerning the civil rights struggle. Thomas had hoped Frank would find a job after college to become more mainstream, but he would have no part of it. He took a job at a community college teaching Afro-American history. Thomas thought his visit with Frank on this trip was going to be interesting now that he had become a Geechee. Maybe Frank could help him research Uncle Jessie.

As Thomas pulled into Frank's driveway, he glanced at the minivan and got depressed. The van was more beat up than Thomas remembered. Frank did not care much about cars. He'd always say, "A to B". This is what a car is for … to get me from A to B. Everything else was conspicuous consumption. Frank thought black folks spent too much money on things that did not matter. He especially went into this lecture when he saw Thomas' car, but he liked to drive it anyway.

This was a surprise visit. Thomas did not call Frank to tell him he was coming because he did not want to use the phone and did not want to call Frank's number using the disposable phones because they might be traced back to him at some point. He knocked on the door and Frank opened and greeted him, "Brother Thomas. What a surprise. I did not recognize you without hair. You shaved your beard too! Now you really look like my twin. Amazing! You caught me. I was heading to class. What brings you all the way from Chi-town to Cleveland? You resemble the Dali Llama."

Thomas said, "Frank, I just needed to get out of the City. I thought a visit with my line brother would be in order."

Frank said, "My house is your house. That is just the way it is. Come on in and get settled. I will be back in a few hours. I see you brought the Mercedes. When are you going to get rid of that car?"

Thomas said, "I'm glad you asked. I need a favor from you. Would you mind if I left my car with you for a few days, and I used your car?"

Frank was puzzled. He said, "Why would you want to drive my hoopty when you have a German status symbol to drive? I need to hear this one, brother. You want to see how the real people live." Thomas knew Frank would give him grief, but that was just Frank.

Thomas said, "Frank, I know this sounds like a strange request, but I'm in a little trouble and need your help. I need to get to Baltimore for Sunday night, but I cannot fly or use credit cards. Therefore, I decided to drive, but the Mercedes is not the car for the trip. I need a car that would not be noticed."

Frank sat down on the hood of the Mercedes, patted the grille, and said, "I'll drive your buggy for a few days. Sounds like you are in over your head, Thomas. If I can help you…you know I got your back. I have to run. We will talk tonight. I'll bring some wine and we can talk it over like back in the old days on the yard." Frank gave Thomas a big hug and handed him the spare keys. He backed the minivan out of the driveway.

Thomas carried his bag into the guest bedroom. The house was a two-bedroom bungalow with a study, built in the 1930's with hardwood floors and arched doorways. Frank was sort of a neat-nick. Everything had its place; his home was exceptionally well ordered. The kitchen was where he spent most of his time. He loved to cook and he had all the tools. Stainless steel appliances, pots and pans, you name it. Thomas knew he would get a good meal, and Frank would help him plan his next move. Frank was much more street wise than Thomas. He worked with youth at risk programs in the City and understood the rules of the street.

Thomas fell asleep on the sofa while looking through a photo album from their first step show as line brothers. Thomas woke with Frank standing over him with his camera planning to snap a picture. This startled Thomas as he jumped up.

Frank said, "Woe...woe brother you're at home. The man does not come to the hood until the trouble is over. Ain't nobody coming here looking for you? Why don't you pour us a glass of Sangria and tell me what's going on?"

Thomas stumbled to his feet, grabbed some glasses, and started to pour the wine. He handed Frank his glass and said. "Why are you still drinking this stuff, why. Why not some scotch or some Crown Royal?"

Frank took his first sip and responded with a smile. "Thomas, that stuff is going to kill you. I plan to live a long life. This vine juice is balanced to keep your Zen in check with your mojo. See me, I am still fit, clear headed and grounded. You go ahead and pour your glass. You weren't too good to drink the vine back in the day."

Thomas said, "I can drink anything. I just thought I would find out why you still drink this cheap wine."

Frank, laughed and said, "Go ahead and talk… you know you still like this wine. Every time you visit, we empty several bottles of this stuff. Speaking of cheap, tell me this: Why do your plates say FORD on the Mercedes? I know that's not your name. Are you too cheap to change the plates?" Frank started laughing and punched Thomas on the shoulder.

Thomas pushed Frank onto the sofa and said, "There is a perfectly logical reason for those plates. I purchased them specifically for the car. You remember my dad, he would always come to visit driving the old Ford Fairlane."

Frank responded, "Yeah, I remember Mr. Jet. He was a cool old dude. The car was old but he kept it clean, always washed and waxed. However, what does this have to do with your dad?"

Thomas responded, "Well Dad did not like foreign cars, and he always said, buy cars made in Detroit because that means jobs for black folks."

Frank said, "Your dad was a righteous dude. He understood the economic linkage to jobs and consumption."

Thomas interrupted Frank saying, "Don't go there with your politics, we are talking about the car's plates. I used some of the money from dad's life insurance to buy the Mercedes. Out of respect for dad, I named the car FORD."

Frank broke out in laughter and yelled, "You've lost it. You need to get out more often… naming a car FORD. Did you name your refrigerator, too? All right, I get it. Your dad was cool. He was okay with me. I guess FORD is okay too."

They drank away the rest of the evening while talking about Nicolette, the boat, the trip to South Carolina and Uncle Jessie. Thomas told Frank about Jessie, the Geechee connection and the need to research his background. Frank said he knew some geechees. He did a research project for one of his classes on the topic of the slave trade and South Carolina.

"The Gullah people are also known as Geechee they were shipped to ports in Charleston and Savannah. They were also shipped to some parts of Brazil from west and central Africa. Wait a minute … did you say your uncle's name was Mande?" said Frank.

Thomas said, "Yes, Mande was his middle name."

Frank said, "Well, one of the tribes shipped to South Carolina during slavery was from the Mande tribe. This may be a coincidence but he or his family may have taken his tribal name after he was freed from slavery. Based on what you've told me this could be one place to start."

After Frank went to bed, Thomas stayed up to do some more research on-line and looked up Gullah, Geechee, and Mande people in Africa. Frank was right there was a connection. Thomas thought aloud, "Does this mean I am Geechee from the Mande tribe? How does this link me to Dr. Oble? Who would care anyway? Jessie is dead."

Thomas woke up at 4:30 in the morning. He'd had another dream about Uncle Jessie. Jessie was sitting on the edge of Frank's front porch looking at him with a frown on his face. He leaned over to him and said, "It's your turn, don't break the chain." Then his body dissolved into dust and blew into the wind. Thomas' T-shirt was soaking wet. He laid awake for a few minutes and then passed out.

The next morning Frank was up early and on the phone and the computer. Frank woke Thomas up with his trademark humor and hangover remedy. He had a glass with a mix of two eggs, Worcestershire, aspirin and soda water in one hand and coffee in the other.

Frank said, "My brother you will enjoy the coffee better if you drink my morning after mixture. This is guaranteed to put your cob webs in order." Thomas' head was throbbing. He would have drunk anything to get the room to stop throbbing. The drink went down quickly. It tasted so bad Thomas forgot about his headache. The coffee was the cure for Thomas. Frank had already made breakfast and had the road maps spread across the table for the trip to Baltimore.

Thomas walked into the kitchen by following the aroma of country ham, pancakes, and grits. His stomach directed him to sit down and grab a plate. Frank announced, "You never could hold your own with the vine. Now that you've told me the real low down about this mysterious trip to the Crab City, I've decided to go with you. I rearranged my classes and I am packed and ready to go. You are going to need someone to watch your back. Besides I would not trust you to drive my hoopty unsupervised."

Thomas muttered his response between bites of ham and grits, "Frank this is not a joy ride. Based on what Jack told me, Dr. Oble is involved with some bad characters, so you do not need to do this. I can handle this." Frank ignored Thomas' comments and went outside, where he busied himself with packing the bags into the van.

Frank returned to the kitchen and said, "Ok, finish up. We need to get on the road because it's going to take seven hours to get there. I want to case the joint before your African see-sayer gets there."

Thomas said, "Frank you don't know what you're getting yourself into. This could be big trouble."

Frank grabbed the cooler while pushing Thomas toward the door, saying, "Thomas, you don't know what trouble is. I am from the Big Easy. I grew up on the streets until I got a free ride to college with my ball handling skills. You helped me get through college and find my life spot. Now, I work with troubled kids. The way I figure it. It is my turn to play it forward and help you. Life is a circle, just accept it, move forward and one hand reaches back to pull another forward."

Thomas said, "That sounds like something you read somewhere."

Frank laughed and said, "Yeah that was pretty good. I need to write that down. I am a genius. I'm going to let you drive the first four hours…"

CHAPTER 4
ON THE RUN

Jack Regis walked up to the door of the cabin. He checked to determine if it had been forced open, and then inspected the window for anything out of place. The cabin belonged to his ex-wife, but it had been awarded to him, as well as the mortgage, after their divorce. She'd kept the house, the cars, and the kids. Jack had not gotten the title changed from his father-in law's name. He thought this would be a safe place to use as a base until he figured out who'd tapped his phones. Located in Maryland near Annapolis, it was not far from the marina where he kept his boat. He did not risk going there until he checked some traps on who may be watching him or Thomas.

The survey of the cabin did not reveal any signs of entry. He set up his laptop on the desk near the window and checked the supplies in the kitchen. While putting away groceries, his phone rang, "Jack, where have you been? I've been looking everywhere for you."

"Rick Dodge …how did you get this number? I just activated this phone four hours ago," Jack responded, surprised, as he scanned outside to determine if he had any visitors.

"You used a credit card to purchase the phone. You're slipping. You've been out of the business too long," responded Rick.

"I like being a civilian. I punched my ticket to get a life with all the trimmings," said Jack.

Rick spoke in a low whisper, "Yeah, I heard about the divorce…sorry that did not work out. How are Jennie and the kids?"

Jack raised his voice, "Enough of the small talk. What do you want and why are you looking for me?"

"Come on, old buddy. Is that any way to speak to an old friend? Your name came up at a security briefing about possible leaks. I thought I would follow up personally," prodded Rick in a patronizing tone.

Jack responded, "I do not know what you're talking about. I left the CIA five years ago. I build things for a living. Check the file in front of you. I'm running my father's development company, that's it."

Rick said softly, "Jack, this is a secure line. Nobody is listening. The leak may not be you, but it is someone you know. You remember Herb Jenkins at the State Department? Herb was running a few projects in a joint program with the National Security Agency (NSA). He got sloppy with some of the security protocols, and he may have gone off the reservation."

Jack said nothing.

"You and Herb go back to your Army days. I thought I would check with you," queried Rick in a yawn.

Jack shouted, "Herb is DEAD! Did you kill him?"

"We had nothing to do with it. We're trying to find out what he was doing, to get some answers about his death," responded Rick.

Jack stood up and walked outside, looking for intruders, before he responded, "Oh, this is just a friendly call about my dead friend. Right! You people poke around and press the buttons to see who runs first. Then you tighten the vice for your quart of blood. I'm not involved."

Rick said, "Jack, Jack, we got the text message to Herbie. You were working with him, looking for information on a diplomat from Ghana. It sounds like you are back in the business to me, old buddy."

Jack responded, "That is nothing. It was just a favor for a friend … a business background check, nothing more."

"Jack, we don't care about this guy from Ghana. He is small bananas. What was Herb was up to?"

"Rick," Jack said, "Herb was a career officer at State, up for retirement in five years. He would not risk putting that in jeopardy."

Rick responded, "Yeah, Yeah. Why did he have $250,000 in small bills in the trunk of his car when he took his swan dive into the Potomac River? That's a lot of cash for a person making G-14 money with a mortgage and kids in college. Wouldn't you say, Jack?"

Jack said nothing.

Rick said, "Okay Jack … well it was good to get caught up on old times. We will be in touch. If anything comes to mind, you have the number to give us a call. See ya old buddy."

Jack slammed the phone on the counter and pulled the battery out of the back. He grumbled, "Herb had $250,000 in cash? Was Herb on the run?" The phone was no good anymore because he knew they were listening. Luckily, Jack had a clean wireless card for his laptop. He could use the internet to make calls on his computer to cover his tracks. Thomas had sent Jack the phone number for his disposable phone to Jack's email address on Youtome.com an internet-dating website.

* * * * *

Dr. Oble had been busy during his six months in the United States. He had not been honest with Thomas when he met him in South Carolina. He had made numerous trips out of DC to meet strangers like Thomas over the past six months and each meeting went the same way. He would meet the stranger, embrace with a hug, say "fufua", and proceed to tell a bizarre story about Africa and seeds of the earth father.

Once while in Houston he'd traveled to an area in Fifth Ward which was known for gangsters, drugs, and violence. He ordered his taxi to stop on Jensen drive, and then he walked for a few blocks to a neighborhood bar. In Texas, they called this particular kind of establishment an icehouse. He went inside in search of a man named Jamal.

Jamal was not like Thomas. Jamal had dropped out of school at the age of sixteen and lived by his own wits. He'd bounced around foster homes until old enough to join the Navy at eighteen. He excelled in the military and liked the discipline. He trained as a Navy Seal, specialized in demolition. Jamal's hobby was free diving; he could dive sixty feet without oxygen tanks.

He was especially proud of this accomplishment, since he could not swim when he joined the Navy. His new career came crashing down on him just before he graduated to become a Seal when he was kicked out of the Navy for stealing whisky from the PX. He proclaimed his innocence but no one listened. He was bitter and never forgot how they railroaded him out of the service. He turned his back on everything and started living the fast life of the streets in Houston.

Jamal, now forty years-old, wore throwback jerseys and a gold grill on his teeth. He'd graduated from being a numbers runner to leading his own gang. The discipline he'd learned in the Navy stayed with him in his new career. His annual revenues were in the seven figures, allowing him to amass a small fortune. Jamal diversified from drugs to prostitution and protection money. Jamal was successful and was shown much respect on the block.

On this day, Dr. Oble wandered into Leroy's Ice House with his cane, wearing a bow tie. He asked the bar man, "Is Ismael here?"

The barman responded, "Mister you're in the wrong place to be looking for anybody. We do not like folks showing up around here asking questions. You better take yourself and that bow tie back where you came from." Just as the barman turned to push him out the door, Jamal, accompanied by his posse, pulled into the driveway in a black on black custom Chrysler 300. The gold plated wheels and grill sparkled. His stereo vibrated the windows in the bar.

Jamal's car was parked near the front door of the icehouse, and just as Dr. Oble stumbled outside, he scratched the hood of Jamal's car with his cane.

Jamal jumped out of his car, clearly intending to pound the barman or Dr. Oble, whomever he could get to first. Jamal turned and closed the car door as Dr. Oble fell to his knees on the ground and said, "Fufua, Ismael, it is you my king!"

Jamal stared at his boys, and then looked at the barman and said, "Who is this old fool? He scratched up my car. Who are you calling king? You don't know me. Get up off your knees!"

Dr. Oble slowly stood up, looked into Jamal's face, and said, "Forgive me your highness. I am a humble man. I see your father in your eyes …he is calling you."

Jamal grabbed the collar of the old man and checked his ID. He yelled and pushed the barman out of the way, as he entered the bar. Dr. Oble followed.

"You are one crazy African. You come into my place acting a fool. Around here, nobody plays me.

I'm the player. I control this block and everyone on it. Yeah I'm the king if you want to call me that, but I'm still going to kick your ass for scratching my car."

Dr. Oble turned around and bent over. He said, "Yes my king, kick my behind, I was wrong to damage your car."

At this point, Jamal said, "Go on old fool…leave now."

"Old great king your people need you. I come from Africa. I had a dream that you would return to help rebuild your nation," said Dr. Oble.

Jamal said, "You don't get it. This is my Africa right here. You are standing in it. I am not from Africa. You need to take your meds. Somebody call 911 and get this old fool out of here."

Dr. Oble picked up his cane and turned to leave, but then stopped. He looked back to Jamal and said, "Your father's, father from Africa was a king. You were chosen to return to lead your people. You must heed this call. It is your time." He left his card with the barman as he brushed off his hat and walked out of the bar.

Jamal glanced around the bar. Everyone was staring at him, as if he were some sort of an African King. He said, "Not a word about this to anyone. If I hear about this old man or this Africa stuff, I will know one of you told something, and I will tear off some body parts until I find out who told." Jamal was not the generous type, and he gave nothing away. He ruled his block through fear and intimidation. This was something he had learned well, growing up on the streets of Houston.

* * * * *

Jack Regis drove into Washington, DC to meet his former boss, J.B. Sutton, from the Agency. Jack's official employment record did not contain any information on his stint at the CIA while he was working for J.B. Sutton. This omission was typical for temporary assignments like Jack's. However, for Jack, this assignment seemed permanent, after five years of chasing spies and terrorist he thought he would never come home. JB Sutton was a career spook. With thirty years and counting, he planned to retire the following year to live in a sailing colony in Barbados. Not the typical company man, JB did not drink or smoke cigarettes, had never married, and his only vice, as far as Jack could tell, was smoking marijuana.

Apparently, JB's parents had smoked pot, and he continued the family tradition. No one would ever believe he was a pothead, except for the fact that he often forgot to clean his fingertips, revealing the tell tale signs of burn residue from a joint. Jack knew JB's secret and from time to time smoked a friendly joint with his former boss.

Now, Jack drove around for forty-five minutes, parked two miles from the metro station, and then walked in circles to determine if he was being followed. The rain had started to fall as he waited on the platform for the red train, then at the last minute as the door closed, he jumped through the door. He did this two more times until he was convinced his tail was clean. Jack finally found JB sitting in a booth in the back of the Life Trends adult bookstore on L Street.

Jack knew this place well. JB had used it as a drop location for instructions for Jack during his last six months on assignment. JB poked Jack in the shoulder with a magazine. He said, "Jack, you need to catch up on your reading. I bought this book especially for you."

Jack pulled off his trench coat and brushed water from his hat. He grabbed the magazine from JB's hand and put it in his pocket. Out of breath, Jack sat down, he said, "Boss, I'm getting too old for this game. I went in so many circles I forgot which train I needed to take to get here."

JB pulled a bottle of water from his briefcase and passed it over to Jack. He said, "You look like you need this more than I do. Let me talk while you catch your breath. I only have twenty minutes before I will be missed at the office. I checked out the folks included in your National Security Agency (NSA) profile."

Jack asked, "What? I've been profiled by the NSA?"

"Yes," responded JB, "but don't get excited. You were always active in their files, even after you left our happy operation. Now here is what they know," JB said, launching into a long report.

"There is a woman named Oshalo Seehwo Erd from Zimbabwe who likes expensive clothes and usually travels alone on a diplomatic passport. She is secretive and suspected to be the daughter of the last living shaman from her tribal area. Like your friend Dr. Oble, she has clairvoyant ability. While living in the US as an exchange student, she worked as an intern on a summer research project with the Smithsonian Museum thirty years ago. Miss Erd stumbled on to her ability to see things in 1985 while working as an analyst at the Smithsonian."

"She completed a psychological questionnaire as part of an application for a position at the State Department. The data on the form indicated she met the profile of a psychic who would be well suited for a special project for the CIA. The job was for the research division for African Affairs. Eventually, she participated in the CIA's remote viewer research project. Miss Erd was the most highly rated candidate for the program. She was a superstar. Her skills exceeded all the initial parameters for the project and as a result the program received a green light for a five-year pilot project."

"Everything worked fine until her dreams started. At first, a nightmare woke her. It was so real she could not tell the difference between the dream and reality. This frightened Miss Erd so much that she was afraid to go to sleep. She feared the program testing had brought on the dreams. Finally, she quit the project, much to the government's disappointment."

"Based on her case file, two years later the dreams came back. According to interview notes, she reported that the space around her would stretch until her dream state took over. She would find herself dressed in tribal robes in a market place in 13th century Zimbabwe. Then she would flash back to the present. The government considered having her committed to a mental facility but her status as a student with diplomatic credentials prevented this from happening. The program was officially shut down in 1990, and we continued to monitor her activities. Historians from the Smithsonian Institute on African studies were consulted on the findings from Erd's visions. They confirmed that the details she had recounted were consistent with the time period she experienced."

"The legend of lost treasure of Great Zimbabwe has swirled around for hundreds of years. Privately, some thought that Erd's visions might be used to solve the puzzle of what happened to Great Zimbabwe. Currently, she is working with the Africa Literary Historical Society (ALHS) as the director of research. The organization is based in Paris with offices London, Ghana, and Johannesburg. Funding for the Society's activities is murky. Anonymous donors are routed through various off shore banks in Switzerland and Cayman Islands, so there is little transparency. This is a dead end. I do not think your trouble is coming from our side. We are watching but the players are visitors. They may be African or European. Frankly, we need a higher body count to determine what we are dealing with."

"Herbie's death may be linked to Dr. Oble. For him to have a large sum of cash with him when he died, he must have been selling secrets. Herb was in charge of sensitive information concerning trade negotiations for oil and mineral rights in Southern Africa. He coordinated security for this project with the NSA. After Herb's death, several files turned up missing. If this information got in the wrong hands it would cost U.S. companies billions of dollars in lost mineral right concessions. What we don't know is, who is responsible for this leak. Thomas Jet missed a fatal plane crash three months ago. NSA was aware that he was coming to Virginia to visit you. Don't be alarmed. They know everything."

"Since 9-1-1 you cannot take a piss in this country without them knowing where and how long. The flight incident investigators found the landing gear tire blew out with the help of a sniper's bullet. The agency prevented any news leak of the story and tracked the passenger list to find a lead. The case was filed as a random terrorist act until Herb ended up at the bottom of the Potomac. His death and Jet's near fatal crash point to your involvement. Jack it is possible there are a few rogue agents in the CIA running a freelance operation, leaking intelligence and industrial espionage, or maybe some contractors went into business for themselves."

Jack asked, "How do I get out from under this?"

JB grinned, "Well you could lead us to Thomas Jet … we'd like to talk to him before he is added to the body count."

Jack responded, "I would not turn him over to you, besides, he's gone under the radar. Let me deal with Thomas."

"Jack!" JB said, "You know how this works, we put out the cheese and watch the rats run. Whomever is watching you, also killed Herb, and is not finished. Now you are the cheese. You remember the Belgian intelligence group that did freelance security work for diamond mining companies?"

"Only vaguely, they were a bloody lot … not much for finesse," Jack rubbed his temple as he responded.

JB pulled out another bottle of water and took a drink and then whispered, "Well this group of likable fellows joined the world of high finance and corporate intelligence through a firm called the International Bureau of Commerce (IBC). If you ask me, they are mostly ex-British Security Service (MI5) types and mercenaries in business suits. They now offer security services in addition to negotiating concessions for mineral extraction services for potential clients. We suspect they negotiate mineral and oil concessions in exchange for weapons for the military. In some cases, they will rent a private army for a coup if the money is right. Unfortunately for their clients by the time they finish extracting the minerals there is nothing left for the government. A few of our people may be in the mix and I suspect they have access to our network. Don't become part of the body count. I'll find you if I get anything that could help. I'll use the usual signal if I need to contact you. I suggest you get some sun and go fishing."

JB picked up his brief case, went out the back door, through the alley, and blended in with the gray suits on L Street. Jack stayed inside until dark, then made his way back to the subway for his round trip to his car.

Safely in the car Jack opened the magazine he had taken from Sutton to find instructions and two marijuana cigarettes tucked into the inside flap. Jack smiled and drove the back roads back to Maryland. He lit one of the joints after setting the sails on his boat and drifted out into the Potomac.

CHAPTER 5
ONE TRIBE

The smoke-filled café roared with the sound of people talking. The room was crowded, with little space to spare for a new customer. No one cared -- it was Paris. Near the window, two men were sitting and staring at a small pottery vase. The vase was colorful and cracked with pieces missing from its apparent repair. They admired the pottery piece as if it were a work of art.

Maalik held it in his hand and said, "One thousand years…. You look at this little broken vase, and think it is a worthless piece of junk. Royce, we are as the pieces mended together. Shattered on the floor it has no form or purpose but put together the vase has a purpose. You can see its beauty." Royce was surprised Maalik showed him the object. Royce thought, *Maalik is a man of mystery.*

Royce was section chief of a covert intelligence unit for a secret organization known as the Brotherhood, based in Johannesburg. Royce sipped his coffee and said, "Maalik, why are pieces missing?"

Maalik responded, "When our group was founded over nine hundred years ago, Ismael Oche broke this clay vase against the floor while the six other members watched. The brothers gathered around as he picked up the broken pieces. The founder said these fragments represented us as individuals from our respective kingdoms. He then asked each member to pick up a piece, and using mending clay, he put the vase back together. When finished, the vase was close to the form we have here today. The founder said this symbol represents our group. The broken pieces represent our people from different kingdoms. The vision from the old king tells us of a threat … not to any individual kingdom or tribe… but to all Africans on our continent. He announced that from this point forward we are one tribe. Everyone there took an oath to keep the dead king's vision a secret and to work to preserve a one-tribe mission. The clay vase and its missing pieces became the symbol of our secret society. The missing pieces represent the souls we seek to help us fulfill our mission."

The miniature vase was three inches tall and fit neatly into the palm of Maalik's hand. Maalik rarely handled the sacred symbol, but on this evening he'd felt compelled to take it with him for his meeting with Royce.

Royce nervously asked, "Why would you carry such a valuable object with you in your pocket. Aren't you concerned it could be broken or worse… lost?"

Maalik sat silent. He thought about Royce's question. "This little vase is only a symbol. It must work like we do, and if it breaks, the pieces will be gathered and put together again. On the other hand, we are links in a chain that cannot be broken. Unlike the vase, our brotherhood embodies generations of links, which are the glue for our collective effort as one tribe, committed to the mission to free Africa," he said.

Maalik tossed a newspaper on the table and read the headline. "Arrests for the failed coup attempt in oil rich African state of Zimbabwe."

Maalik asked Royce, "Did you see this article about the arrest of European mercenaries? This is another blatant attack on our continent. We must make more progress in Zimbabwe."

Royce responded, "Yes we are tracking the story but this coup was thwarted. This is good news. Our so-called European friends are still responsible for many of Africa's problems."

Maalik leaned over to whisper, "Tell me about your meeting with Erd. I am aware she met with you last week. She is our most valued recruit from Zimbabwe. We found her in the United States." He pulled a map of southern Africa from his brief case to show Royce where his field agents where working. Concerned about security Royce did not use the map provided by Maalik, instead he folded it up into the newspaper and passed it back to him.

Royce responded, "Yes. I reviewed her portfolio. Erd did not have much use for small talk. I briefed her on the status of our operations. We have agents working leads on a plot to bribe the government in a neighboring country to allow a major oil company to steal millions of barrels of oil.

The civil war in central Africa left several diamond and gold mines in the control of a militia funded by a French conglomerate. Our agents are there, tracking the flow of diamonds and gold out of the country. Erd agreed to use her clairvoyant abilities to help us follow the money flow. to gather additional information to expose those behind this scheme to the United Nations' oversight committee on corrupt practices and organized crime. She left abruptly after we broke for lunch. She mentioned something about finding the missing link."

"We must not fail to expose these criminals. Erd will deliver soon. Keep me informed." Maalik raised his cup and made a toast, "To Africa and good hunting." . He put the vase in his pocket and the map in his brief case. With his cane in hand, Maalik weaved through the café patrons and out to the street.

Royce sat there for a few minutes and reflected on the frail old man as he walked away. He had been recruited to join the brotherhood five years ago. After a brief stint in British Secret Intelligence Service (MI6), his last job was director of security for diamond mines in Sierra Leone. Royce had witnessed firsthand what was happening to African nation states. Since the first independent state of Ghana to the Congo, Europeans had meddled and undermined African governments. They provided arms for coups and when that did not work, assassinations were common.

Royce was not surprised about the news of the recent coup arrests. The news of prominent people from Europe being involved was nothing new to him. Africa was a dangerous place where the rules changed without notice.

The brotherhood has had many names over the past nine hundred years. Before the Europeans arrived, they were simply called "Moja Kabila" or "One Tribe". Some called the group a cult. Others in the west referred to them as a secret society like the Skulls & Bones. By any name, they existed. African freedom was the core belief of the group. The brotherhood began when a king of a small nation near Ghana had a vision of the demise of his country and all others like his. The king summoned the high priest of his court to study his vision. He sent seven emissaries to other kingdoms to share his concern about a cataclysmic event that would ravage the continent and end Black African rule, as they knew it. The old king foresaw the holocaust that would kill hundreds of millions of Africans, cause wholesale destruction of generations of written history and culture, and bring humiliation to the entire race of Africans from Egypt to Great Zimbabwe.

The vision focused on the African Diaspora, where millions of descendants from the continent would be spread out in large numbers in distant lands west to the Americas. The king spoke of the great link to the old Africans in the other world to the west and the seven clans. The vision ended with Africa's rebirth in the twelfth year of the new millennium.

The king reached out to other African Kingdoms to share with his vision, which returned for seven years until the king's death. Emissaries from several African nations came to show respects at the death of the old king of this small country. No one believed the old king's vision. It was impossible to comprehend that foreign invaders would dominate all of Africa.

The emissaries witnessed a collective vision as the king's body burned. The king appeared at the end of the vision saying, "We must prepare for the rebirth of the Continent." This spiritual experience was the beginning of the Moja Kabila (one tribe). The men gathered around the burning remains of the king, stunned by the images of the vision. Individually, they acknowledged they would be no more successful than he in warning of the impending destruction of their world. Each emissary went back to his country and pledged a solemn oath not to reveal the vision. They formed the nucleus of the original founders of the Brotherhood, a secret society committed to prepare for what was to come. Each member agreed to recruit seven individuals from the court of the king of their respective nations. They swore a blood oath only share the contents of the vision within the group.

The timing of Africa's devastation was not determinative, but the shaman for the dead king predicted the signs. The first sign would be the sacking and burning of Timbuktu. Preservation of history and culture was the primary mission of each chapter of the brotherhood. Each would establish a process to retain the histories of each kingdom through practices that would conceal their existence. The preservation of tribal history transmitted through oral histories passed from generation to generation.

The brotherhood perfected a process that could compress one hundred years of history into four hours, through chants and meditation. The process-required selection of a special subject called a traveler, who possessed the spiritual and psychological gifts to retain the messages. The security feature of the process was that once the histories were transferred to the traveler's memory, a third person would say a few key phrases to lock the data. This same procedure is used to retrieve information. The traveler would not remember the uploaded information in their active memory. Hypnotists used this technique to help people remember or forget, to diet or stop smoking. This procedure was similar. It protected the traveler, and the brotherhood in the event security was compromised. Without the key, the secret was safe. Over time, the role of the traveler became a generational responsibility of the first and last-born. Before he or she died, they passed on the information to the children of the next generation.

After the fifth generation of the existence of the brotherhood, the changes started to unfold, as the old king's shaman had predicted. The African slave trade with the west was the next sign. Brotherhood members were kidnapped into slavery and eventually an entire community in West Africa was captured and enslaved. The slave trade and the colonization of Africa disrupted the organization.

Maalik's family in Mali had been forced to flee to Turkey. Brotherhood members who survived preserved oral histories left by descendants of the original seven dating back to the eleventh century.

Royce had been recruited, like Erd, by Maalik. Royce did not have Erd's psychic gift, but he was committed. Secrecy was the key to the brotherhood's survival. Anyone who was exposed soon disappeared. Royce's meeting with Erd was also concerning information leaked about her operations in DC.

* * * * *

Twenty years ago, Maalik traveled to the Congo to map the location of selected sites based on Erd's visions. After arriving, he contracted with mercenaries in order to excavate treasure that he uncovered and transport it to Lebanon for sale. The diamonds that he located were valued at $50 million, but on the black market, Maalik netted only half the real value.

The mercenaries received a fifteen percent cut for their efforts, but unknown to Maalik at the time, an intelligence agent named Fieldon, who actually worked for the International Bureau of Commerce (IBC) got involved. Since that time, the IBC had been trying to find out how Maalik learned of the location of the ancient artifacts that had been hidden away for hundreds of years. The IBC had been tracking Maalik's movements ever since.

CHAPTER 6
THE MEETING

Back in Washington, DC, Dr. Oble was pacing the floor of a hanger reserved for international flights at Washington National airport. He had been waiting for forty-five minutes, when finally a sleek Lear jet taxied inside. Lights flashing from the nose landing gear showed brightly through his glasses. Unfazed by the noise and lights, he stared straight ahead with an intense focus. He waited patiently while the ground crew prepared the passengers to disembark from the plane.

The early morning 3:30 a.m. arrival assured that no one would be around the hangar except the ground crew and the transport limousine. The driver, a tall ex-military type, wore a black suit and carried the extra padding in his clothing of a bulletproof vest. From his expressionless face, Dr. Oble could tell that the man had done this before. After the stairway was lowered, a slender female figure descended the steps onto the hanger floor. She had a small frame and a tight waist. Her face was hidden behind a hat with a wide brim. She waved to Dr. Oble and quickly slipped into the waiting car, disappearing behind the tinted glass. The driver approached Dr. Oble, patted him down, and then used a wand device to check him for weapons or other electronic devices.

Dr. Oble stood patiently erect while the man patted him down and checked for security. The driver tapped him on the head to indicate his passenger was clean. The woman motioned for Dr. Oble to join her. Once seated inside, the car and its two passengers sped away quietly in the night.

Dr. Oble did not speak. Finally, after a few minutes of silence the woman said, "Do you have something for me?"

He responded, "My good lady, I have accomplished my assigned tasks to the detail." He handed her a flash drive without any other comment. She placed the drive in a netbook. The device flashed and data appeared on the screen.

She smiled and said, "Dr. Oble, you do good work." He reached into his jacket pocket, pulled out a flask, and poured her a drink, using a small silver cup.

He poured a drink for himself, raised his glass, and said. "Miss Erd, here is to the future. May the chain never be broken."

She smiled again, drank a sip, tapped the window for the driver, and said, "This is your stop. I will contact you with your next assignment. Aren't you headed to Baltimore?" He nodded, yes and gathered his cane, exited the car and disappeared into the night. Erd continued her journey, heading south to McLean Virginia.

* * * * *

Frank drove the last two hours into Baltimore. He was familiar with Baltimore having spent summer visits there at his aunt's house. The van came to a stop at Reene's Crab House near the dockworker's union hall on Press Street. Frank woke up Thomas. They tumbled out of the vehicle and pushed through the swinging doors. Renée's was a shack with a bar, wooden plank floors, picnic table, and benches. The tables were covered with newspaper, and beer was served in metal buckets. The place smelled of crabs and beer. Thomas stopped at a payphone in the hall while Frank ordered three dozen large crabs and six beers. By the time Thomas got to the table, a dozen crab shells were piled in front of Frank, and half the beer had been consumed.

Frank never looked up at Thomas. He focused on finding meat in the crab claws. Frank grunted, "Thomas, I knew you would be a while so I went ahead and ordered my crabs. You can have a few of these, but you need to order some for yourself."

Thomas laughed while opening a beer. He took a long drink and said, "Ahhh! This takes me back to the old days on the yard when we would take a road trip. There is nothing like the first beer when you get to where you're going."

Frank pushed aside the pile of empty crab shells and said, "Too bad we have to leave here to meet some old African. Otherwise we'd be headed out to the club tonight."

Thomas put down his beer and reached over, picked a crab, and joined the feast.

After the crabs were finished, Frank put on his glasses and looked at the map, eager to find the hotel. He said, "The hotel is twenty minutes away. We have three hours before we need to meet the African. Let's go over to the university library. It's a few blocks from the hotel and I want to do some research on your uncle. Driving through Pittsburgh I had an idea about where to look for information on Jessie. This may help when we meet the African."

Thomas agreed that the more they knew, the better. He was concerned that Jack had not contacted him yet, but he did not let Frank know this part of the story.

Frank wanted to check the county court house in Charleston for records on Jessie. He hit pay dirt in the marriage records when he discovered that Jessie had married in 1906. The license indicated that he was born in the Congo in 1878. Frank found baptismal records posted at the Charleston genealogical society, and the record indicated that a Negro preacher named Joshua Goddard, who did missionary work in Africa, had adopted Jessie while there. He brought Jessie, a nine-year old boy, back to the States when he returned to South Carolina. Frank had become an expert at genealogy research by helping his students find their roots. He'd taught a course on the topic during the last summer session. Frank printed several pages from the web site. He and Thomas finished the research and continued their journey to the hotel to meet Dr. Oble.

Thomas sat looking out the windshield, thinking he would never be the same again, now knowing his father was from the Congo.

I am really an African, he thought. He sat in shock, watching the rain pound on the windshield. Frank grabbed a coke from the cooler and went on talking about Jessie and how exciting this search had become.

"Thomas," Frank said laughing. "Just imagine your next family reunion when you go to Africa. Don't look shocked … every black man in America is a descendent from Africa. You're lucky you can trace your direct link to Africa through your uncle Jessie, I mean your father. I had to do a DNA test to find my genealogical link to Africa."

"Nobody is trying to kill you," replied Thomas.

"Well, you've got a point there," said Frank.

Thomas did not respond. He just stared out the window. Frank parked the van outside the hotel on the street at a parking meter in case they needed to make a quick exit.

Thomas' phone rang just as they approached the hotel entrance. He answered and found Jack was on the line.

"Thomas, finally, I've been trying to call you for hours. You need to be especially careful. Remember your rough plane landing with the blown tire? It was not an accident. My contacts do not know who is responsible but they have connected the dots to you, Herb and Dr. Oble. I decided to take the boat for a sail to get some distance from the situation until we can figure out what's going on."

Thomas started breathing faster. He whispered, "Okay this makes my day…I'm in Baltimore getting ready to meet Dr. Oble to get some answers."

Jack responded, "He and Erd are interesting characters. They are connected to an African research society. Psychics and remote viewing underworld, not sure what, but it sounds serious enough to be killed for. You need to watch your back. They tell me it is not our side pushing the buttons since Herb's death. Herb had $250,000 in his brief case. The best I can figure is when Herb pulled the profile on Dr. Oble it cued someone who was tipped on you and me."

Thomas responded, "Jack, thanks for your help. The more I move, the deeper I sink in the quicksand. Call me in the morning. I've got to go."

* * * * *

The heat was unbearable; the sun was high in the noon sky but no one seemed to mind inside the bar. It was summer in Houston. August was the hottest month, but ask anyone in July, and they would say that month was the worst.

Jamal sat sipping on a glass of beer while staring at the screen on his laptop.

Few people knew that he was going to night school at the community college and studying business. He kept this to himself, thinking his crew would not understand. Jamal understood the power of knowledge and the need to know how the system worked. The news was full of gang leaders mismanaging money, being arrested, losing their cars, houses, and cash. Jamal was determined this would not happen to him. Jamal planned to clean his money through legitimate businesses. He had been on his way to purchase his second apartment building when the old African scratched his car.

Jamal never got the scratch fixed on his car. Every time he looked at it he thought about the ramblings of Dr. Oble and his talk about Jamal being a descendant of an African king. He remembered the African saying, "Become who you will be." After the encounter, Jamal had a series of dreams, and some took place in what he thought was Africa, but not in the current time. The dreams were vivid --filled with people he did not know but who seemed familiar to him. The colors and smells from his dreams still lingered in his mind. He had never dreamed about Africa before, and the dreams felt so real he could not stop thinking about them.

Jamal was careful not to discuss any of this with his crew for fear they would see this as a sign of weakness. Instead, he spoke to his history professor at the community college where he attended night school. He told his professor about the dreams and inquired if there was a possibility of life continuation from another time. As his professor was from Nigeria, Jamal thought another African might have some insight. His professor had studied in the United Kingdom at Oxford. He told Jamal about Friedrich

Nietzsche's philosophy and his doctrine of eternal recurrence.

The professor explained Nietzsche's philosophy, that time or life was part of a cycle that was repeated many times until a correction was made. Jamal asked his professor if he thought time travel was possible. His reply was not yes or no, but rather vague.

He said, "In my village at home in Nigeria we have a tribal elder who believes he is from another time and there are those in my tribe who believe him and rely upon on him for advice and counsel. I am a university trained professional and I understand these folk tales cannot be proven, but the elder's visions and wisdom have always been uncanny and incredibly accurate." He went on the say, "The world is full of mysteries. Man would like to think he has all the answers, but I must admit I believe our village elder, too."

The professor wrote down the name of a book for Jamal to read on the topic and walked Jamal to the door of his classroom. He patted Jamal on his back and said, "Son, keep an open mind. The eternal hourglass of existence is turned upside down again and again, and you with it, speck of dust." This was a quote from Nietzsche. His professor smiled and walked backed to his desk to prepare for his next class.

Jamal pondered what he had heard about Nietzsche's philosophy and thought, What if the blacks taken from Africa are experiencing this *eternal* return but cannot make the correction because slavery disrupted the natural life cycle of the entire continent. Could it be possible that the dreams and the old African are part of the re-ordering of things? He thought for a few moments then shook his head and said, "This is too deep for me."

Jamal got busy and researched eternal recurrence as well as the possibility that his dreams were about past lives of his descendants in Africa. After the seventh night of the same dream, Jamal could not ignore it any longer and finally decided to call the old African. Jamal got the business card the African had left with the barman at the icehouse and dialed the number. The voice on phone said, "Hello your majesty. I hoped you would call."

Jamal said, "Yo who is this? I'm calling to speak to the African. Is this Doc Obleee...?"

Dr. Oble responded, "Yes this is. I am glad you called. Now you know who you are. Have you seen your future yet?"

Jamal yelled, "Yo... I don't know who or what you are, but I want you to take this hex off me. I am going to break your legs in three places, if you do not get this off me....You feel me!"

Dr. Oble responded, "Great king, I have not the power to take from you what is already yours. You are seeing your future and this is not for me to change. I am only your humble servant."

Jamal became agitated and fired back, "Ok, I'm going to go along with you. I need to meet you. Where are you? I communicate better in person."

"Your brothers are meeting me in Baltimore on Sunday at seven o'clock7PM at the Inter-Harbor hotel. Come there and I will answer all of your questions." Dr. Oble terminated the phone call. Jamal called back several times but no one answered.

Jamal felt his life changing. He was afraid to go to sleep because the dreams were getting more and more intense. He knew the key had to be the African. He was determined to get back to normal and to his business. He could not sleep. He could not focus. He had to go to Baltimore.

At the airport, Jamal, who had never flown before, paced the floor, waiting to board his plane, watching passengers deplaning at the gate. He noticed how casual everyone seemed about flying. People were coming and going as if they were at the bus station. He wondered how people could be so calm after flying at thirty thousand feet for three hours. Did they understand how dangerous this flying thing was? He shook his head and continued to pace the floor. Finally, they called his seat number for boarding, and he started to sweat. Through force of will he walked down the gateway, boarded the plane and found his seat. After the plane took off, he settled down and slept until the captain announced the plane was preparing to land.

Jamal looked around the plane and noticed that everyone was calm. He left the plane got his stride back and strolled up the jet way, acting as if he had flown hundreds of times. As he got into the cab, he thought, *This was nothing for a king and I will own a jet before I'm done.*

Jamal found the hotel and checked in, hoping to get some sleep before he met with the African to put an end to the dreams.

* * * * *

The hotel had seen better days. The bar's dark wood panels and leather chairs were the setting for karaoke night. The bar was full of regulars and the stage was set up for the talent contest. Frank entered the bar and scanned the faces, looking for the African, but had no success. He bought a beer and sat at the back of the bar, intent to wait and watch for possible threats to Thomas. As he kept an eye on activity through the mirror behind the bar, he saw two men walk up to the bar and take the two seats on either side of him. Frank got nervous and ordered another beer. The man to his left started a conversation with Frank by asking, "Brother, you here for the contest?"

Frank responded, "Yes, I'm here to drink and watch the show."

The man responded, "Yeah, interesting…the show is always better when everyone participates."

Frank said, "Yo... you're right, but I don't sing."

The man responded, "I don't sing either but this is not why I'm here, *Frank*."

Frank took a big gulp from his beer, turned to look at the man and said, "Well since you know my name what's yours?"

The man stood up, extended his hand, and said, "Brother Eric Kingsley from Morgan State." He gave

Frank the secret handshake to verify his membership in his fraternity. He said, "I met you at the East Coast Meets West Coast step show three years ago." Then, Eric introduced Nate, who was sitting on the other side of Frank. Frank breathed a sigh of relief, settled in for the evening with the brothers and had another beer.

By 7PM, the bar had become crowded with locals and talent wannabes waiting for their chance at stardom at the microphone. After about an hour Jamal walked in the bar area, looking for the African, and finally settled in at the bar, sitting across from Frank. By 9PM, no African had shown, and the talent show was winding down to the last songbird singing *The Impossible Dream*. Frank was almost asleep when the bartender announced, "That African is not coming to the bar tonight if anyone is interested. He will be here tomorrow."

Frank noticed Jamal and several other men appeared to be disgusted that the mystery man was a no show.

As Jamal prepared to leave the bar, Frank approached him and asked, "You here to see the African, too?"

Jamal looked at Frank, pulled his jacket over his shoulder and grunted, "What's it to you? You are looking for that old fool, too!"

Frank responded, "Brother, I'm here with a friend who is supposed to meet him here, but I've never met him before. I heard he is a strange dude."

Jamal warmed up some to Frank and said, "Yeah, he is something different. I don't know him, either. He bumped into me and scratched my car."

Puzzled, Frank said, "I'm not trying to pry into your business but did you come here to get him to fix your car?"

Jamal looked at Frank and grabbed his collar. He said, "I don't know you, but I don't roll like that. If I wanted to get him, I would have put him down where I found him. I take care of my business."

Startled by Jamal grabbing him, Frank said, "Yo... brother I'm not hating. I'm just trying to learn more about the African."

Jamal pulled back and said, "Hey man, I'm not sweating you, I just wanted to let you know I don't roll like that. I'm a man of action. I'm here to see the African to get some answers. He is some kind of witch doctor or spirit man. I met him once and he changed my life. I want my life back. This is why I'm here."

"Let's have another beer and talk about this," Frank offered.

Jamal shrugged, and ordered another round of beers.

Frank sat down in the booth across from the bar. When Jamal came back with the beers Frank told Jamal that he was there for the same reason. For the next hour, they talked about Jamal's experience in Houston. Frank and Jamal looked around the bar and wondered aloud if there were other people in the bar to meet the African. They exchanged mobile numbers and agreed to meet in the afternoon to plan for their meeting with the African.

Thomas, who did not go into the bar, waited in the restaurant for a signal from Frank to let him know if the African showed up. Frank left Jamal in the bar and went to the restaurant to find Thomas to compare notes on the African and his conversation with Jamal.

Thomas was drinking a scotch when Frank walked up. He said, "Frank, I am enjoying this quiet time with my old friend."

Frank picked up Thomas' glass and drank it down. Thomas was shocked at Frank drinking his drink. Frank said, "Don't be tripping, I need a strong drink after Karaoke and your African adventure."

Thomas said, "You never came to get me. I thought he did not show."

Frank ordered another scotch and said; "Yeah right… but there's more. The bartender announced around nine o'clock that the African will be here tomorrow night, but this is not the big news. There are others like you. I met a gangster named Jamal, who had a story similar to yours. He is nothing like you. He is straight from the street like some of the brothers I used to run with in New Orleans. He was packing, he is a big guy used to running things. He is a long way from home…. Houston."

Thomas sipped his drink and said, "Houston, huh. The African gets around. What is he up to…?"

Frank cut Thomas off. "Jamal told me about how he met Dr. Oble and about having dreams that won't stop."

Thomas listened, stood up to order another drink, but then paused. He said, "You know I started having strange dreams right before I left Chicago. I thought it was stress from this mess but now it sounds like it is connected to the African, Jessie, and now this Jamal. What does it mean?"

Frank pulled out his wallet and paid the check, then said, "It means you're in some deep shit. Let's get out of here and find a hotel. I need to get some sleep. "

Thomas finished his ice and grabbed his jacket. He and Frank walked out the back door of the bar and left through the parking garage just in case someone was watching.

* * * * *

They were watching. Parked on the side street across from the hotel was a white van with the sign General Janitorial and Carpet Cleaning. Inside were two men sitting in a cramped space wearing headsets with monitors and recording equipment. Gene Simpson was a contractor. He was always paid in cash and hired through a third party. Gene never knew who he worked for and did not care as long as the cash was there. The envelope with information about the assignment had been left in a trashcan outside the Metro stop at Union Station. Gene was accustomed to secret money drops with unknown clients. He liked not knowing any more than he needed to know. The bag had five thousand dollars with instructions for him to wire the hotel bar with audio and video devices and record the bar patrons' conversations. The target was the African and anyone with whom he met. Gene had the African's picture taped on the monitor. Empty coffee cups were scattered on the floor of the van. Gene was not neat; he weighed three hundred pounds and wore thick glasses. His partner Clifford was a thin small man with a baldhead. bald head. He was Gene's unemployed brother in-law. Clifford was not very smart but he was loyal and always needed money.

Gene's cameras were on a remote control and could span the bar, the sitting area and the stage. He got pictures of Frank, Jamal and everyone else, but no African. He recorded the barman's announcement that the African would be at the bar tomorrow night. He needed to be paid for another night's work if they were going to get the pictures he'd contracted for. Without the African, all the other pictures he had taken had no value. His contract promised him another ten thousand dollars if he got the African's contacts at the bar. Gene called his contact to report his progress.

The phone rang for two seconds before the voice on the other end said, "Talk to me."

Gene responded, "We have a no show. The African did not make an appearance. We have pictures of everyone there but none with the subject. The bartender made an announcement that the African would be at the bar tomorrow."

The man on the other end of the phone said, "Scan and up load the pictures from the bar to the email address on the money envelope. Your money for tomorrow's work will be at the same place after you deliver the pictures with the African."

"You will have the pictures within the hour. Is the bonus still in place?" Gene responded as sweat rolled down his head into his coffee cup.

The man responded, "You're lucky I did not pull the plug on this job. If you deliver, we will deliver."

Gene hung up the phone, lit a cigarette, cussing muttering to himself. Clifford fidgeted with the monitor, sensing the money for the job might be in jeopardy. He asked, "What's the plan?"

Gene threw a half-eaten doughnut on the floor and yelled, "We need to get the African on film with his contacts. Scan and up load the pictures we took tonight and send them to the email address on this envelope. I'm going to get some food because we need to spend another day here to wait for the African."

The voice on the phone was Rick Dodge. Dr. Oble's phone transcript had given Rick the hotel bar information for the meeting. Rick had tried to convince Jack Regis to give up information on Thomas but with no success.

Rick Dodge was an ex-CIA agent who ran a freelance intelligence operation. Rick had experience with African intelligence from his days in Angola, Congo, and Uganda as a military attaché at the US embassy in Ghana. His clients include the CIA, his former employer. His official business was a company called Acme an import export business based in New York with offices in London and Brussels. Acme offices were located in Brooklyn in a nondescript building with no signage just the address 5050. Acme traded in coffee and copper but also dealt in information and special projects for the CIA and anyone else who would pay, even the International Bureau of Commerce.

Officially, folks in Washington did not want to publicize any interest in the car accident that led to Herb's demise but the CIA wanted to know about his connection to Dr. Oble and the source of the two hundred and fifty thousand dollars. To find out about Herb, the missing records and the money, all roads led to Dr. Oble, Thomas Jet and maybe even Jack Regis. The CIA passed on this assignment to Rick after the death of Herbert Jenkins.

In unofficial Washington, Thomas Jet was the subject of much interest. Fortunately, for Thomas, his senses were becoming more in tune with the shadowy world he had been forced to enter.

* * * * *

The night after the no show at the bar Thomas had another dream. This time it was not about Jessie or his father. It contained a speaking voice like Dr. Oble's. The voice said Thomas was to wake up and listen to his message. It sounded like an echo in his head. Thomas got up, went to the bathroom and splashed water on his face, but the voice did not go away. It finally, stopped then started back by saying, "Jessie, now isn't this better than mobile phones."

Thomas said, "Dr. Oble, is this your voice in my head?"

"Yes, son. It is not safe to use the phones any more. I need you to meet me tonight at Rock Creek Park near the north entrance at the bike trail near the rest area. Do not tell anyone, not even your friend, Frank," responded the African. The voice went silent and the echo was gone. Thomas sat on the side of the bed and thought, *Yes, that was him. Nobody would ever believe what just happened.* He kept this secret and did not tell Frank. Instead, he asked Frank to go ahead to the bar to meet the African, telling him he needed to go meet his friend Jack Regis. He did not think Frank would believe him anyway. Thomas took the minivan and Frank took a taxi to the bar.

Thomas drove to the park. As he walked down to the creek, he thought about the strange dreams and his father not being who he thought he was. He heard voices in his head. *I must be going crazy,* he thought. Then to his surprise, he saw six other men gathered at the meeting place. They were standing around the bench. Thomas walked up the hill. A tall man approached him from behind and asked, "Did you hear the voice too?"

Thomas responded, "Yes, I heard the voice last night."

"Where is the African?" the man asked. "My name is Jamal. We all got here at the same time but the African has not shown himself."

The men gathered around the bench and introduced themselves. Everyone stood silent for a moment, and then heard the sound of a drum coming from across the creek. Jamal walked close to the creek to investigate. He shouted, "There's a camp fire over here and the African must be beating the drum."

Thomas and the other men crossed the bridge that spanned the creek and followed Jamal to the campfire. The drum stopped. Then the African appeared from behind the trees. Dr. Oble was dressed in a silk robe, gold in color trimmed with green and red designs on the sleeves and at the bottom. His head was covered with a hood and his hands held a gold rod with inlaid diamonds and emeralds on the tip. He made a striking entrance, looking like a king, and much different from the bow tie wearing professor whom everyone had met earlier.

Around the campfire were seven bundles neatly placed at precise spacing around burning logs. Dr. Oble raised his scepter and directed each man to stand before a specific bundle. Jamal attempted to say something but could not. He stuttered, then finally gave up and moved to his place around the fire. Jamal had seen the campfire the man in the gold robes and the golden scepter before in his dreams. Jamal felt he had been here before.

With everyone in place, the African spoke, "Fufua my fellow travelers welcome home. Fufua means 'awaken' in Swahili. I know you have many questions about your dreams. However, first we must respect the elder spirits that brought us together. You have journeyed a long way to learn answers to many questions. Now you have reached the beginning of your next life. After we finish giving honor to the founders you will have all of your questions answered."

Dr. Oble proceeded to present each man with a robe similar to his, but different. All the robes were made of silk woven with gold braids. The sleeves had different color combinations. He assisted each man with his robe. Once the brothers were all attired properly he spoke in a different African dialect for each brother, using language that no one understood. He pulled a silk pouch from his sleeve, took a pinch of sparkly dust and flecked the dust on the fire.

He said, "I have a message to share with you, as it was told to me sixty years ago. The ancestors of our clan are from a long line of keepers of our history and secrets. Repeat after me the names of the founders; Techehi, Maliche, Lechie, Domari, Nayenah, Isamael, and Alameh." The African walked around the circle and placed a gold ring with emerald and ruby stones on their index fingers. The African said, "This ring is a symbol of your connection to the great link of brothers in our Tribe of One."

The African took a small dagger from his pocket, sliced his finger and passed the dagger to each man gathered around the fire. Following the African's example, the brothers sliced their fingers, then the group joined fingers together over the fire. After this final ritual was complete Dr. Oble said, "You are now links in the chain that cannot be broken. You will keep our secrets until death or the afterlife. Long live a free Africa!"

Thomas, Jamal, and the rest of the men came from around the fire and inspected their rings, the robes and each other.

Dr. Oble announced, "Time is growing near for you to open the door to your memories to learn your role in your new life. Your next life begins today. You have powers that you have not discovered yet. You seven represent the sons of the lost tribe stolen from mother Africa hundreds of years ago. After today, your dreams will become more frequent and clearer. In time you will be able to communicate telepathically with the others in this group as I spoke to you last night. My job was to help you awaken and to bring you together as a group. It is now for you to organize and find your own way. I can tell you that you are not alone … there are others like you all over the world. Some have been awake for generations, preparing for your arrival. Others are like you becoming awakened and finding their way. There are evil forces working against Africa and its descendants. These forces have been at work for many generations and continue today. The founder said in the beginning that in the seventh year of the new millennium the sons of the lost tribe would rise and bring greatness back to mother Africa. In your bundle, you will find a mobile phone for you to use for communication with each other. For your protection do not use these phones for any purpose other than communications within the group."

After the ceremony everyone stood in shock except for Thomas, who asked, "Why me? Why now?"

The African smiled and nodded to Thomas and said, "You were selected before you were born. Your role was cast generations ago. The prophecy is clear that after the seventh year of the new millennium the descendents of the lost tribe will be awakened. It's your turn to take your place to change the world."

"Hey, I have a life in Houston, I got things to do!" shouted Jamal.

The African said, "You asked to see me. That is why I am here. You can do what you please. What is awake in you now has always been there. I simply provided you the key. The scepter will guide you." The African asked the men to gather in a circle around the fire; he chanted a few words, then threw the pouch in the fire. The fire produced a lavender colored smoke with the smell of lilac. He continued to chant until they went into a trance-like state while staring into the fire. The vision of the old king reappeared for a few moments and the brothers around the fire shared the vision and their collective thoughts.

Dr. Oble said, "You are now a part of the great link with your fellow travelers around the world that are joined in the struggle to free Africa." The men stood in a daze for a few moments. Then the African vanished into the darkness.

For several minutes, they stood there looking at each other. Then a portly fellow in the group spoke up and said, "My name is Goode. The African placed the scepter in my hand so I guess I have drawn the long straw to get us started. I like you, do not understand what just happened. As one of the seven, if what we have learned today is true we have a responsibility to understand what it is before us. Before we leave here we need to see if this voice-mind-link thing works, then establish a plan if we need to meet as a group again."

One by one, they tried to communicate using their thoughts and slowly they connected with everyone in the group. This was almost like a religious experience for the men, which bonded them together as one. Dr. Oble told them the mind link initially would only work when they were close in proximity but over time as they grew stronger the link would work over long distances.

Thomas told the group about his suspicions that the government was investigating him and Dr. Oble. Jamal sat with his hands over his eyes, confused and distraught. Thomas patted him on his shoulder and said, "Brother, I feel you. This is some kind a strange magic and we need to stick together to see this through."

Jamal stood up and suddenly pushed Thomas to the ground. He yelled, "You don't understand. I run the streets back in Houston. I am not right for all of this voodoo African stuff. I came here to end this, not to begin something new. All you people beaming thoughts into my head, strange dreams, I cannot do this." He pulled his gun and put it to his head. He pulled the trigger. Nothing happened. The gun jammed. Goode wrestled the gun away from him.

Thomas tried to calm Jamal down by saying, "Look around you. Everyone here did not want to come but was compelled by something within. Simon is a CEO of a fortune 500 company. Glenn is a minister with a church down in Oxford, Mississippi. Luther was homeless until last year. Dawson is a petroleum engineer. Pete is a professional gambler. The dreams and the voices came to all of us. No one here has all the answers. We cannot continue our lives as they were and ignore what is happening to us. This is why we are here. No one chooses from whom we were born to or what family we came from. We now need to decide how we will live after this experience. We all face the same crossroad here. If the old African is telling us the truth our choices after this moment not only affect us, but our place in history."

Jamal sat down, nodded his head, and said, "I'm a stand up man. I do not back down. You are right about one thing, today is a beginning. I made myself into the king of my block in Fifth Ward and can master this thing too and change the world." Jamal grabbed his gun from Goode and put it back in his waistband. He gave Thomas a bear hug, and said, "I will stand up and hold up my link in the chain. We seven have a job to do." The group agreed to meet again in thirty days. All communications with the new phones would go through Goode first, then to Jamal and so on. With this last detail, the group embraced and parted as brothers with a blood pledge of secrecy.

CHAPTER 7

"ERD"

The sun was bright in the southern sky. Under a sweltering sun, bumper-to-bumper traffic moved slowly. The driver glanced back at his passenger as she motioned for him to keep going. Miss Erd was on the move again, traveling around Brazil, going from Sao Paulo to Rio de Janeiro for three days. She was on her way to the airport; she had been busy since her meeting with Dr. Oble when he reported on his contacts in the U. S. and Canada. His contact with Thomas and his fellow brothers was the final step to activate the brotherhood in North America.

Erd had never married or seriously dated since finding out about her psychic gift. Tempted on several occasions she always came back to the thought of too many secrets. Her life had become too complex for civilians to understand. She remembered how she used to live one day at a time, open to the surprises and challenges each day brought. Now she lived for the past and the future. Time had little meaning anymore. Erd could sense what the next day would bring. She was aware that there was a war for the heart of Africa underway.

Since the fall of apartheid in South Africa, the battle had intensified and the stakes had increased.

The ability to glimpse the future made living for today meaningless for her. It had been thirty years since she discovered her place in the brotherhood. She rebelled at first, then became resigned to the reality that her duty required total commitment to the mission. According to the prophecy, time was running short. Travelers were awakening from generations of sleep, many separated from reprogramming for more than two generations, leaving their roles to be determined by free will and remembrance. Erd's job was to coordinate awakenings for those in the Americas and the Caribbean. This was her third visit to Brazil and she had failed to locate the final contact.

Zek was traveling with her on this trip. Erd had introduced Zek to the brotherhood five years earlier in Sao Paulo. Growing up in Brazil, he felt the weight of prejudice. Zek was ready to give up and leave the country when Erd awakened him to his new role in the brotherhood. Since then Zek worked to organize the brothers in Brazil. He hoped self-consciousness of Blacks in Brazil would increase to the point they would demand true civil and economic rights as citizens. He believed a free Africa would help inspire his brothers and sisters in Brazil to seek access to more opportunities at home.

They finally arrived at the airport. As the car pulled into the hanger, an elderly man watched from the shadows. When Erd exited the car, he tapped his cane and she saw it was Maalik. She muttered, "Why is he here....?"

Maalik gazed up at the ceiling and started to chant. "Hummumid, Hummumid, Hummumid...Erd.... Hummumid."

Erd stopped and closed her eyes. Maalik grasped her hand, and together they boarded the plane. She said nothing until Maalik spoke.

He said, "My child our time is running short. The prophet instructed that our preparations must be complete by the 12th year of the new millennium. I gave you the last key, now you have all you need to complete the chain. You have three full moons to find the last link in the Americas to complete the chain."

"I will not fail you," responded Erd.

Maalik interrupted, "Child, this is not only me sitting here. I embody the will of generations which guided us to this point, now we must perform."

"I understand," whispered Erd.

He winked at her as the pilot taxied the plane to take off. Erd smiled and settled in for the flight to Jamaica. Maalik placed his cane on the edge of the chair and proceeded to tell his story. She had heard rumors about Maalik's generational line but not the actual story. They had met on three occasions but this one would be different. He was one of only a few travelers who could track his family line through ten generations.

Maalik's family line began in Mali. His Mandingo ancestor saw a vision of his tribe being decimated by an attack from Moroccans. The voice in his vision told him this was not his time to die. He was directed to move to Nubia and finally to Constantinople which is current day Istanbul. They stayed there until 1946 when his family moved to Europe then on to Paris. The first and last-born continued to pass the secret for more than eight hundred years.

Maalik told Erd his work was done and no more people from his line would continue the link of the chain. When he took his last breath ten generations of his line would die with him. The weight of this knowledge was a tremendous burden on him. As a result, Maalik started carrying the little vase with him to remind him of those he carried with him on his journey. He placed the vase in Erd's hand during the flight to Jamaica.

This trip was magical for her. The tiny vase, the original symbol of the brotherhood and the old man, heightened her senses. Erd was fast asleep when the plane landed, and she woke feeling her spirit renewed. The old man waved her farewell as she departed, but he stayed aboard the plane and flew back to Paris.

* * * * *

Jack Regis's sailboat ended its journey in Jamaica. He had decided to take an extended vacation while sorting out the reasons why the agency had chosen him as a person of interest. JB, his old boss, had sent him a message stating Jamaica was a good place to start to search for answers. JB tracked Erd's flight plan to Jamaica. He suggested Jack find her to seek information about Herb Jenkins to determine if he had been selling state secrets.

Erd checked into the Royal Palm hotel in Montego Bay. She always traveled under assumed names to conceal her movements. Jack had no problem finding her; he waited for an opportunity to approach her. He watched the hotel lobby and checked with his old contacts at the embassy to learn if he had made the watch list in Jamaica. He bought a mobile phone on the street to stay off the grid. Finally, he was ready to make his move; Erd was walking toward the café. Jack approached her and asked, "Do you have the time?"

She checked her watch then turned to him and said, "Who cares about the time, this is Jamaica. What do you want Mr. Regis?"

Jack was surprised she knew his name. He stuttered, "You're good. I heard about your psychic ability, but now I have witnessed it firsthand. Why don't you join me for a cup of coffee? Call me Jack, my bill collectors call me Mr. Regis."

Erd said, "Come, let me buy you a cup of coffee. You have many questions for me." She smiled and got to business, "What do you want, Jack?"

He hoped for more small talk but Erd had no use for polite conversation. Jack responded, "I'm in a bind, the Feds are listening to my phones, following me around, and I think it has something to do with Dr. Oble. A friend of mine, Thomas Jet, asked me to check out Dr. Oble a few months ago. My contact at the State Department named Herb did me this favor and found himself at the bottom of the Potomac River."

She stared into his eyes for a few moments. She responded, "This has nothing to do with my business. I represent the African Literary Historical Society. We do not deal in state secrets."

Jack ordered another coffee, scratched his head, then asked, "Can you point me in the right direction? Maybe this is linked to your work." Erd finished her coffee and prepared to pay the check.

Jack grabbed her hand. He said, "Thomas and I are tangled into something we do not understand. Can you help us?"

Erd smiled and pushed his hand away. She responded, "Thomas will find his way. If you choose to dig into this further you can start with IBC."

"What is the IBC?"

"The International Bureau of Commerce is based in Belgium, with representatives in D.C. and New York. They plan to remake the world if you believe their literature. Commerce without borders, free trade capitalism will solve the world's problems," explained Erd.

Jack asked, "Why are they interested in your work in history?"

Erd picked up her purse to walk away. She said, "Jack you're pretty bright, history is the key to the future. If you study carefully, it will tell you everything you need to know."

Jack reached out to touch her hand. At that moment, he felt a slight vibration, and Erd disappeared. He looked around to see where she had gone. He rubbed his eyes, thinking it was impossible for her to vanish. He thought, *that was some strong coffee*. He looked at his wrist and noticed his watch had stopped. He sat for a few minutes and then decided to retrace his steps from where he'd met her in the lobby. Jack reached down to tie his shoe and was shocked to see Erd lying on the floor.

She was shivering and hyperventilating, unable to breathe. Jack leaped over to her and lifted her in his arms. She could not speak. Jack found her room key in her purse and carried her to her room. She said nothing. He was shocked to see her again so quickly. *How could she disappear and reappear?* he thought. He laid her down on the sofa and put a blanket over her shoulders. She lay silent for about an hour, whispering to herself until finally she recognized Jack, who was sitting in the chair.

Erd sat up. "How did you get in my room?"

Jack smiled and said, "If I answer your question are you going to tell me how you disappeared into thin air in the café?"

Erd shook her head. She said, "Did I really disappear?"

Jack responded, "Yes for a few minutes. We were talking and then you were gone. I was getting ready to leave the café and begin to retrace my steps, then you appeared on the floor, shivering as if you had been to the Arctic Circle. What's going on?"

Erd became somber after listening to Jack's description of her vanishing act. She took his hand and asked questions concerning his family and background. Erd wanted to learn more about him. He gave her what she asked for, hoping she would tell him what he wanted. She asked how he'd met Thomas. After learning more she said, "Are you the one?"

"Hey wait a minute. What do you mean the one? My phones are tapped and someone is watching me. I need to know what's going on. Yeah, I'm the one with the target on my back," responded Jack.

Erd said, "They may not be aware of who you really are, but they know you are connected to us. At the Café, I remember talking to you, then a bright light blinded me. I found myself in Africa. I think Zimbabwe, not as it is today but maybe as it would have been five hundred years ago. I could make out the castle from a distance. I've experienced visions like this before but this one was more real, as if I were actually there. My clothes were from another time. I spoke a different language. I did not know for sure what was happening until you told me you actually saw me disappear. This had never happened to me before. I was gone longer than a few minutes … it seemed like several days. I lived in a village near a large lake. I did not speak, for fear my words would betray me. The village was under constant threat of attack from foreign invaders. The men had left to go to join the battle with warriors from the great castle. Just as the horns were sounding to warn of a new attack, the bright light appeared. You were sitting across from me in my hotel room. My study of the ancient history of Zimbabwe leads me to believe I traveled back to this place."

"You don't recall lying on the floor in the café or me carrying you to your room?" Questioned Jack.

"No, Jack," responded Erd. "I remember the village and the old lady who took care of me. I thought I was dreaming. It felt real, but impossible. We have opened the door to the beginning. You are part of my link to the past. I have been looking for you for the last ten years."

Jack sat expressionless, rubbing his eyes to make sure he understood what was going on. He said, "I'm going to the bar to order a tall glass of scotch. I am going to enjoy my cocktail and return to my boat. This is too much information on an empty stomach. If I wake up in the morning and remember all of this, I will know this is real, otherwise I'll just assume this never happened."

Jack grabbed his sunglasses to walk toward the door.

Erd hummed and held his hand as he walked. She said, "Mr. Jack, when you wake in the morning you will find your life has changed as my life-transformed years ago. I am glad you found me. I will be waiting for you." Erd kissed his lips and said, "Good night."

Jack pushed the button in the elevator, thinking nobody would ever believe what just happened. He walked up to the lobby bar and told the bartender, "I need a tall drink of scotch and no ice."

When he awakened the next morning, the previous night was a blur. Jack scanned his boat and wondered how he'd gotten back to the marina and into his bed. He checked the mirror to inspect the damage from his night of drinking. He heard someone on the deck, so he grabbed his baseball bat. As he crept up the stairs, he smelled coffee. To his surprise, Erd was standing by the rail with a cup of coffee in her hand.

Jack said, "You again. I thought I was dreaming, am I dreaming? Did you bring me back to my boat?"

Erd smiled and handed Jack a cup of coffee. She said, "Good morning Mr. Jack, I told you I would be here in the morning."

"You mean," Jack pointed his hand toward the hotel.

"Yes…it happened…it's real and I'm here." She prepared breakfast and asked him to sit while she served him her special dish. She explained how they are connected.

After her disappearance, she had asked Jack about his background. He'd explained he was from Virginia, and his father passed away ten years ago. His mother was a mulatto from Rio. He and his father emigrated from Brazil. His father changed his name from Galibis to Regis because it sounded more American. Jack had an olive complexion. In America, being from Brazil, he and his father were considered Hispanic for all practical purposes.

Jack took another bite of food and said, "Are you telling me I am not who I think I am?"

"No, you are who you are, color does not define you. I just explained how I missed you in my search. Your color means nothing to me. Your blood and your family line are what make you special to me. Apparently others are also interested, Galibis is a Berber name. Did you know Berbers lived in Timbuktu and Mali? You know this is in Africa, right. Yes, there were white people in Africa one thousand years ago. We are connected, you will see."

Jack sipped his coffee, and then said, "You are wrong. The spooks are snooping around because my friend Herb pulled a report on Dr. Oble. He's caught up into something, this is how we are connected … nothing else."

Erd gazed into Jack's eyes and smiled. She kissed his lips. She said, "You really don't get it do you? This is not about your friend Herb. He may have stumbled onto something, but I suspect the IBC is the cause of your problem. He discovered the link between you, Thomas and Dr. Oble."

Jack asked, "Why terminate your own asset."

"We don't know who killed him," responded Erd.

"I've been in the CIA, military intelligence, and out in the private sector for years and no one ever came after me until now. What's so special about me?"

Erd touch his hand. She said, "You are the key to the treasure. What happened yesterday is a game changer. There are no coincidences in our business.

The IBC understands this all too well. They are worthy opponents."

"I didn't vanish, you did," said Jack.

Erd responded, "Yes, this is true, but you had to be the catalyst to open the door, and this has never happened before. IBC has psychics on their payroll. They know we are close to a breakthrough."

Jack pushed back from the bench and said, "If we keep talking about this, I'm going to need a drink."

Erd laughed, "It's not so bad… it just takes a little while to get used to your new life."

Jack said, "What new life? I have a life already in Virginia. I have a thriving development business, too."

"Yes you do, and now you have the brotherhood. We are connected as you are to Thomas," responded Erd.

Jack said, "Thomas is my friend. He saved my life twice during the Gulf War. This is why we are connected."

"Have you ever thought he was placed in your life to save you for a greater purpose? We are all connected in some way. Sometimes it never becomes clear. You've known Thomas longer than you think. The brotherhood is a secret society. You cannot join. Membership is by birthright, unless one of the seven recruits you. The group is based on the original seven whose family line can be traced back to the 11th century," responded Erd.

He shook his head. "If it's such a secret, why are you telling me?"

"Jack it's my duty to tell you. The prophet told me when I found you, I should disclose everything. You are a descendant of one of the seven. It is your decision what you do next. The secret is yours to keep. Of course, getting someone to believe you may be a challenge, it is entirely up to you. If you tell the wrong person it could be terminal. I know after you've had a chance to sleep on it you will do the right thing."

She leaned over and kissed Jack on his cheek. "I have to return to the home office with news of the event and inform them that I have found you. I will contact you when I finish my business there. We will see what the future holds for us."

Erd left the boat and climbed into a car parked outside of the marina gate. The car sped away before Jack realized he had no way to contact her. He sat on the bench facing his boat. He mused, "Did this really happen? No one would believe this story…I am not sure I believe it."

Jack went to the cabin to connect his computer with the wireless card he'd purchased in the market. He found an envelope with his name on it and inside was a round trip ticket to Johannesburg, ten thousand dollars in cash, a mobile phone, and a note from Erd.

He read the note: "Yes, it happened, otherwise you would not be reading this letter." Jack smiled and read on. "Now that I have your attention, we need your help. You may not accept everything that has happened but you must at least be curious. If you want to learn more, take the challenge and travel to Africa. When you arrive, call this number and our representative will brief you on the situation and everything will become clearer."

At the bottom of the package was a gold ring set with emerald and diamond stones. Jack examined the ring closely and thought, *This is a nice piece.* He put the ring on his finger. It fit perfectly. He said, "Okay. Ok. I am hooked. I guess am going to Johannesburg to look for some answers and get my life back."

* * * * *

Erd's mind held memories that dated back more than five hundred years.. Unlike Dr. Oble, she had effectively tapped into most of the secrets she held. During the last twenty years, she had cataloged oral histories and down loaded most of the records. One secret held in her memory was the location of treasure from the lost empire of Great Zimbabwe. Erd was looking forward to finding the last key that could unlock the mystery. The missing link was believed to be in the Americas.

CHAPTER 8

THE TRIP HOME

Thomas was prepared to drive the last leg of the trip back to Cleveland, feeling okay about not meeting the African at the bar. Thomas had told Frank nothing about his meeting with his newfound brotherhood because the blood oath he had taken forbade telling anyone. He knew Frank had noticed the band-aid on Thomas' finger and his new ring but had said nothing about it.

Frank asked, "What are you going to do next?"

Thomas finished packing his bag for his trip home. He announced, "I need to get back to Chicago and unwind my life to determine what fits. The African, Uncle Jessie and my past will take time to work through. I decided to take an extended leave from work. As for the spooks spying on me, I cannot live in fear. If someone wants to listen to my conversation, I have nothing to hide. I've not committed any crimes against the state or anyone else. I need to get on with living." Thomas gave Frank a big bear hug and threw his bag in the back of the car.

Frank leaned against the car. He said, "Great road trip just like back in the day. Brother, you have changed on this trip. I cannot put my finger on it, but you turned the corner on your discovery of who you are. I think you're really the African's son." He slid his passport out of his pocket and put it in Thomas' hand.

Frank said, "I need some stamps in my passport. We look like twins, with your new haircut. Take this with you when you see the world. I am a land lover so make me look like an international traveler. I will report my passport lost in a few months. If I cannot drive to it, I'm not going. Just like Madden with the bus."

"I can't take your passport," responded Thomas

Frank said, "Brother, no one is looking for me. If you need to disappear use it."

He was right. Thomas nodded. He started the car and backed out the driveway. He yelled out of the window, "Power to the people, I'll see you next time."

* * * * *

Thomas arrived in Chicago with a different perspective. His first stop was Aunt Maggie's house. Thomas followed the walkway to the garden. Fall leaves covered the ground. He found Maggie sitting on her favorite bench reading a letter.

Thomas said, "Hello Aunt Maggie, I saw your car in the driveway and I thought I'd stop in to visit."

Maggie ran over to Thomas and gave him a big hug. She said, "Son, I prayed you would come home to me. I got worried when I could not reach you on the phone. Your office would not tell me where you went. Those men came to my door looking for you and I got scared just thinking about your father, Jessie."

"I could not call you. You said some men came here looking for me?" asked Thomas.

"Yes, are you hungry? I made dinner earlier so let me warm up something for you to eat. Do not say anything? Come with me to the kitchen," replied Maggie.

Maggie walked up the path to the house. Thomas followed her, worried about the strange visitors. He was looking forward to a home cooked meal. As she pulled food from the refrigerator, Thomas asked, "Who were they?"

She reached for her apron from the hook on the door and wrapped the pull strings around her, then looked out the window. Maggie said, "I remember five years after your father, and Jessie, came to Chicago two men came to my door. They drove a long black car, wore hats like in the gangster movies, flashed their badges and claimed to be government agents. They asked about Jessie and showed me an old picture of him. I was scared. They pushed their way into my house, moving from room to room, looking for Jessie. I blurted out, 'He's dead. He died last year.' I gave them the name of the hospital where Jessie died and the funeral home that buried him. Abruptly, the men turned around, thanked me for the information and left as quickly as they came. I did not sleep for weeks. I never told your father about their visit. He had his hands full raising you and working, besides they never asked about you, they only wanted Jessie."

Maggie turned the oven on and placed a black pot on the stove. She emptied greens into the pot and started to hum as she focused on the meal.

Thomas asked, "What about the men who came looking for me?"

Maggie started crying. She said, "I'm sorry, baby, I did not know what to say. They claimed to be federal agents doing a routine background check on your company. They looked just like those men from thirty years ago, I did not tell them anything. They flashed their ID badges, but I could hardly read their names. They were here last Monday."

Thomas stared at the ceiling as Maggie spoke. He thought, *Monday was when I met with the brotherhood.* He said, "Aunt Maggie it's okay. I've done nothing wrong …if they need to find me, they can."

Maggie fixed a plate for Thomas and placed it on the kitchen table. Thomas began to eat as Maggie sat down and watched him. She said, "I love to watch you eat my cooking… you always seem to enjoy yourself. I need to tell you something I've been holding back all these years."

Thomas asked, "What's wrong?"

She pulled a book from a nearby shelf and showed Thomas a piece of paper. The paper was a letter with letterhead from a law firm located in Washington, D.C. Maggie started crying again. She said, "I got this letter a week after your father and

Jessie arrived in Chicago. It explained that I had inherited a small fortune from someone I did not know. The benefactor wished to remain anonymous. The law firm of Bittle, Brass & Boyd was contracted to administer this part of the estate to Margaret Swanson. The letter stated any attempt to find out the name of the benefactor would result in the termination of the monthly payments."

"Every month for the last thirty-five years they sent me a check. I quit my job, purchased this house, and had a life I had never known before. After your father and Jessie showed up, I had more than I needed, and so I helped whenever your father would let me. After Jessie died, the payments increased from five thousand to seven thousand dollars per month. This is when I knew the money was connected to you in some way. When your father became ill and knew he was dying. He told me what Jessie told him when he agreed to raise you as his own. He said Jessie told him of a vision where he saw the world change. He said you had a part to play. I had never seen your father look so intense than when he told me of Jessie's vision. He said we are all connected. The hair on the back of my neck tingled."

Thomas nodded, finishing his last bite. He said, "Auntie, he was right. I cannot tell you more. Nothing happens without some purpose. It is for us to find the meaning. This is why I stopped by tonight, to tell you I've found a new purpose for my life."

Maggie hugged Thomas, and said, "You go do what you need to do."

"I will be leaving Chicago soon and may not see you for a while. My business partners will take over the practice until I can come back to work. The less you know the better, in case those men return," responded Thomas.

* * * * *

Jamal arrived in Houston. At baggage claim, he grabbed his bag and walked out to his car in the parking garage. He drove home, looking around his neighborhood with a different point of view. His mind kept flashing back to the old African and his new brotherhood of secrecy. He glanced at his hand where he'd cut his finger as part of the blood oath and knew it had really happened. He felt different now and wondered, *How does this change how I handle my business? I am still the king of the block, I run things here.*

He pulled into the parking lot of the icehouse bar. Jamal felt a pain in his arm. When he walked into the bar, everyone stopped talking. His number two man, Rudd walked up to him and placed a roll of cash in his hand.

Rudd said, "Yo... boss, here's the take from the weekend. It's only ten thousand, the corner was slow."

Jamal took the cash and pulled one thousand dollars off the roll, "Take this to the youth center and give it to the do gooders for the kids. From this day forward, we are giving back to the community from our pot. If any of you got side hustles I do not know about you had better give ten percent of your money to the youth center … just like you see me doing right here. If I hear about money not getting there, I'm taking everything."

Ruud asked, "Why are we giving up our money to the chumps? We take, we don't give."

Jamal pushed Ruud to the ground and pulled out his walking stick. Ruud backed up against the bar, thinking the stick would soon be meeting his head, but Jamal did not use it.

Instead, Jamal said, "This is good for business. We take care of the community it will take care of us."

Ruud got back on his feet and said, "Okay boss. I will get this done."

Jamal left the bar and got into his car. As he drove off, he thought *I am not the same as before.* He looked at the roll of money and realized his future was changing. He had thirty days to sort out his life before the next meeting of the brotherhood. He could not do that while running his block. He had a decision to make.

* * * * *

In New York, Simon was also struggling with his newfound connection to the brotherhood. He was accustomed to being the only black in corporate settings and as a result, he thought of himself as special. Simon lived in a bubble where most of his friends were not black. He struggled with connecting with blacks in professional situations.

After returning from the meeting in Rock Creek Park, Simon felt he had changed. His first week back at work left him feeling unfulfilled and he questioned whether his work brought any value to the world. His company routinely earned millions in profits but that was not enough anymore.

Simon decided to attend his college homecoming weekend for the first time since graduation. He contacted some of his old classmates and found the address of Buford, his best friend from college. The train ride from New York to Boston gave him plenty of time to think. Simon had lost touch with Buford but he knew his old friend was going to be a mover and shaker. He remembered where Buford's mother lived, so he stopped by, hoping Buford would be in town for the festivities. He knocked on the door. A man in a wheel chair greeted him. It was Buford.

Simon did not recognize him at first and then he looked closely at his face. "It's me, Simon, I thought I'd come hang out with you this weekend."

Buford was happy to see him. "I'm not hanging out much," he said. "I am not as mobile as I was in college. Mom died last year and now my sister lives here with me. I was just going down to the store … you want to walk with me?"

Simon responded, "Sure. I just got in town. I'd like to look around the old neighborhood."

Buford powered his wheel chair through the door, down the ramp and on to the sidewalk. As

Simon walked behind him, he thought, *What's going on here? I cannot believe this happened to Buford.*

Buford stopped at the red light and waited for the light to change. He said, "You've been gone quite a while. I had planned to go to LA to work for a public relations firm but my dad got sick and mom needed me to help her. Therefore, I delayed building my empire. I read about you in the Business Journal and followed your career moves. We are very proud of you brother, I thought I would be up there with you. I was shot fifteen years ago while I was sitting on my mother's front porch. Now my plans are deferred for good."

Simon smiled and nodded as they walked into the corner market. Simon looked around the store and became uneasy. He noticed a woman with pink hair, wearing short shorts who was hanging around the beer cooler. She had yellowish eyes – clear signs of drug use. Buford purchased two, forty-ounce beers and some cigarettes. Simon helped by carrying the beer and opening the door.

Buford shouted, "I don't need any help. I come down here every day by myself just fine. I can get the door!" Simon was taken aback by his comment, stepped back as Buford pushed the door open, and rolled out to the sidewalk.

As the two men waited at the red light, nothing was said. A car pulled up to the corner and a woman yelled at Buford, "Are you crazy coming down here? Yale Street is dangerous. There was another drive by shooting right where you are standing last night. You need to get your ass home." The car sped off as the light changed. Buford looked up at Simon and laughed. "You are out of your element. Not like you remembered, is it? Crack cocaine ruined this neighborhood."

Buford stopped his wheel chair and pointed across the street to a boarded up apartment building where they had been roommates in college. "Look over there!" he shouted. "The flood of crack cocaine turned this place into a drug den. It used to be safe to walk the streets. Now you take your life in your hand to walk to the store." Simon nervously looked around, trying not to appear frightened.

Buford reached into the bag on the side of his wheel chair and showed Simon his gun. He said, "Don't worry, they know me around here. I don't go anywhere without this anymore. This is what the "man" is doing to our community with this crack stuff. If I had my legs, I would do something about it. The so-called war on drugs is all about putting black men in jail. Don't mind my sister, she is always on the warpath. She feels like she is stuck here with me, but really it's the other way around."

Simon started walking with Buford. Nothing was said until they got back to his house. Simon knelt down, hugged Buford and said, "My friend, you're right. I'm a little out of touch. I came here thinking about how it used to be but instead I see how things have changed. If you ever need me, call me." Simon shook his hand, gave him his business card, left the porch and got into his car. He knew Buford was too proud to call him but if he ever did call, Simon would help him. Simon drove around the campus and the old neighborhood.

All the streets around the campus were named after Ivy League schools like Harvard, Princeton and even Yale, where Simon had attended graduate school. The city planners probably thought those street names would inspire residents to high achievement but Yale Street was the most dangerous street in the city. Simon attended the homecoming and later boarded the train for his trip home. He kept thinking about Yale Street and how it had changed. He thought, *It takes more than lofty names and symbols to make changes.*

Two weeks before the brotherhood was scheduled to meet again, Simon started thinking about what they could do as a group. The dreams had started to come more frequently and the meanings had become clearer. While Simon was shaving, it came to him what to do…they needed a place to think, work and study the dreams to understand what actions they needed to take. Simon thought if the others were having the same problem as he, the status quo would not work as a long-term solution.

Simon went to work. He drafted an outline for the framework of a study group on Afro American and African development. He put out some feelers to find funding for a nonprofit research group. The next day Simon received a call from an attorney with the law firm of Bittle, Brass & Boyd. He had never heard of the firm before but the representative explained that he represented a client who wished to remain anonymous. They had an interest in providing exclusive funding for his group. The lawyer explained that Simon's reputation was the reason they contacted him. The lawyer said he had secured a funding commitment for five million dollars for the yet to be named organization. Simon was puzzled by the call and the offer. He promised to get back with the firm after he discussed the generous offer with his colleagues. For the next two weeks, Simon worked on the details of his plan with his financial advisors and attorneys.

* * * * *

Goode, another member of the brotherhood, was back in Seattle in court for a four-day trial. He was an attorney who specialized in medical malpractice litigation. He enjoyed his work. Except now he found it difficult to concentrate.

One problem was the scepter Dr. Oble gave him. He wondered why he had been chosen to be the keeper of the scepter. Every time he held it, he could feel a slight vibration tugging him forward. He was afraid to keep it at his house for fear of losing it if his house were burglarized. Goode was not an expert on ancient artifacts but he knew the object was solid gold and the diamonds were real. He put it in his pool cue carrying case and into his safety deposit box for safekeeping. This was the only way he could sleep at night. Having responsibility for the scepter prompted Goode to volunteer to be the point person to coordinate with the group.

From the time he was a child until he graduated from law school Goode had always been a leader. He was captain of his football team, president of his class and editor of the law review. He took to leadership like a fish to water, as his grandmother would say. She raised him and taught him to take responsibility for his actions. Law school was a natural for him; he loved public speaking and debate. He knew if ever he was to run for elected office, law school would prepare him. His father was dead and his mother was a drug addict. His mother had left Goode on his grandmother's porch when he was a baby. He never thought of his parents. His grandmother smothered him with love and discipline. Goode never had time to feel sorry for himself.

His grandma was from New York and was a big fan of Marcus Garvey. She preached self-reliance morning, noon and night. Goode had his own heroes but his grandmother stood out as the most influential person in his life.

After the final oral arguments, the jury had the case for deliberation so Goode took a deep breath. He said to himself, "This is not fun anymore." He had heard similar sentiments from his fellow brothers of secrecy. Goode had communicated with all of the brothers. He had not thought about his situation until he finished the trial. When the jury came back with a favorable verdict, he thanked them and left the courthouse, wondering if he would ever do this again. The following week he would be traveling to the meeting place to compare notes with the brothers to determine his next step.

* * * * *

In Atlanta, Luke had not slept through the night since leaving the park in D.C. with his new African brothers. Luke's life was full of challenges. Luke joined the Marines after high school and served in the first Iraq war. He earned the rank of Gunnery Sargent and had been destined to be a career soldier until he became ill after he returned to the States. He found himself discharged after his medical condition kept him so fatigued he could not perform his duty assignments.

Luke returned to his hometown of New Orleans to look for work and start his life over. He trained as a chef at the Fairmont Hotel and discovered he had a knack for cooking and creating new dishes. He left the hotel and opened a cafe that showed signs of promise. Then hurricane Katrina washed away the city and his life.

Luke was homeless for six months until finally he moved to Atlanta and got a new start. Just when Luke got back on his feet, Dr. Oble stumbled into his life and turned it upside down. The damage from the hurricane changed his life in a profound way. Always proud of America and his service in the Marines, Luke became disillusioned and bitter. Luke called Goode often. Goode assured Luke that things would be sorted out when the brotherhood met again.

CHAPTER 9
THE CHASE

It was midnight and the winter season brought its usual nasty weather to Brussels. Frederick Eddington had just returned to Brussels from Maryland. He was glad to be back home even with the freezing rain pounding against his face. He thought coming home would not be right without a little unpleasant weather. His car had not arrived. He stood with his hulking frame erect in the cold, waiting, his frail hands shaking, holding a cigarette. A black limousine pulled to the curb. The driver jumped out and hurriedly opened the car door for him and placed the bags in the trunk.

He had dark circles around his eyes, he was a chain smoker. Eddington always had a cigarette in his hand -- either one he'd just finished or was preparing to smoke. Light blue cigarette butts littered every place he had been. He was particularly irritated because he had to fly on a commercial flight that would not allow him to smoke. The driver knew Eddington would be in a foul mood.

Once in the car, Eddington complained about the untidy appearance of the vehicle and the driver's lateness in picking him up. He informed the driver that for his being five minutes late that he would dock him a day's pay. He reminded him that his immigration papers were not in order. Eddington said, "Just one phone call from me and you will be on a boat back to the slum in Estonia."

The driver did not try to explain but simply looked at his boss through the rearview mirror as he closed the privacy glass. Eddington did not like excuses. If the driver said anything, he would have made the call with no hesitation.

Mr. Eddington was director of security for Mideast and African operations of the International Bureau of Commerce (IBC). His foul mood began in the States when his operative Gene Simpson had failed to capture Dr. Oble alive.

Gene Simpson had picked up Dr. Oble's trail when he returned to his apartment in Washington. Gene had received his assignment at the usual place at Union Station in D.C. The envelope was thicker than normal, he was excited about a big payday. He found ten thousand dollars in crisp one hundred dollar bills and the promise of twenty five thousand more after he delivered the package.

Gene was accustomed to jobs where no questions were asked. He knew if he started asking questions the assignments would stop coming his way. He had not done a snatch and grab solo before so he brought his always-needy brother in-law Clifford along on this job. Clifford was a small time thief but never did anything physical like assault. They staked out Dr. Oble's apartment building and followed him to the alley behind the Metro station.

Clifford grabbed the African from behind. Dr. Oble began to yell. In a panic, Clifford began to choke Dr. Oble to shut his mouth but his chokehold had a more permanent effect. They left his body on the street and turned his pockets out to make his death look like another D.C. mugging. Witnesses reported seeing Gene's van and provided the license number to Metro police, along with a description of Clifford.

The situation was quickly turning into a disaster that could expose the IBC. Eddington had to call in a few favors to clean up the mess. D.C. park police found the bodies of Gene and Clifford in their van, lying at the bottom of the Potomac River. For good measure, Dr.Oble's wallet and passport had been planted in the van, along with other stolen items to close the case and end the trail to IBC. The number of bodies found in the Potomac was starting to grow. The police were satisfied, so they closed the case but Jack's friends at the CIA were not.

Eddington's office in Brussels was located in a nondescript building in the warehouse district. The limo driver blew the horn at the gate and the garage door opened. As he drove inside, a woman named Cecily, armed with a hand full of files, greeted Eddington and handed him a mobile phone. She said, "It's Rick Dodge in New York." As he talked on the phone, she escorted him upstairs to his office. The driver breathed a sigh of relief, happy that nothing else was said about him.

The plaque on the wall in Eddington's office read, "Presented to Major General Peter Eddington for 50 years of loyal service to Force Publique." It was his father's award for service to the Belgium government as commander of an elite division of the Congo's police. Frederick did not follow his father's career path, but instead, joined the Foreign Service. He worked at the embassy as the military attaché after the Congo gained its independence from Belgium. He joined the IBC in 1970 and worked his way up to his current position as security director. He never talked about what he did while at the embassy but he left the service with high-level contacts in the KGB and CIA.

Chaos is good. The IBC started every day with that mantra for intelligence operations in Africa. The post-colonial Africa strategy for Western interests and IBC clients was focused on maintaining control of mineral resources.

The assassinations like that of Patrice Lumumba in the Congo became the road map for the West's Africa strategy. Left in the aftermath was a brutal dictator named Mobuto and fifty years of disorder and destruction for the Congo nation. Throughout this dark period foreign mineral mining interests continued to operate.

Intelligence agencies like the IBC used the chaos strategy to undermine governments in order to maintain control of Africa's resources. The IBC employed mercenaries to protect mining operations for clients while at the same time planting seeds of discontent with groups that worked to destabilize the region. If the host government was fighting an insurgency, they couldn't focus on controlling mineral resources. The resulting chaos left the IBC and their clients in control of diamonds, gold, copper, and other vital natural resources.

IBC's official business specialized in mining and oil concessions in developing countries. Their clients were secretly vetted before being approached with opportunities. Eddington's interest in Dr. Oble had started with an investigation to find the source of security leaks that resulted in a failed coup attempt. The leak caused the IBC to lose over one billion Euros in concessions on a huge oil find. Dr. Oble was linked to the person suspected to have blown the whistle on the coup. He disappeared from Johannesburg and resurfaced in Washington DC six months later. The suspected whistle blower's nude, dismembered body was found with cigar burns on the torso. The unrecognizable head with the left ear missing was discovered in an alley in downtown Johannesburg.

With Dr. Oble's death, Eddington was not any closer to finding the source of the leak but he was now searching for Thomas Jet and Jack Regis, for they were possible targets to finding answers. IBC agents were in Chicago looking for Thomas. Jack's boat was located in Montego Bay, Jamaica but the trail was cold.

Unknown to Eddington, Dr. Oble's real reason for traveling to South Africa was to search for a missing manuscript from Timbuktu. News reports of finding thousands of manuscripts in Timbuktu dating back to the 13th and 14th century had created renewed interest in history once thought lost in Africa. The

South African government agreed to fund efforts to preserve recovered manuscripts for the Mali government.

The brotherhood was searching for a mysterious document believed to be a clue to the lost diamond treasure of Mali. Dr. Oble's mission had been to retrieve the document. He served a brief stint as a visiting professor at the University of Cape Town where manuscripts from Timbuktu were translated and preserved for the Mali government. While visiting Johannesburg he had befriended a diplomat from Zimbabwe. Dr. Oble helped his new friend quit smoking through hypnosis but much to his surprise his new friend, while under hypnosis, told him of Eddington's plan for a coup d'état of the Zimbabwean government.

Dr. Oble successfully retrieved the missing manuscript from the university archive. Before leaving Johannesburg, he secretly passed the information about the coup conspirators to officials in South Africa. Upon his arrival in D.C., he presented Erd with the missing manuscript that contained the clues for the location of the lost diamonds from Mali. He neglected to mention the other business of the coup attempt in his report.

CHAPTER 10

THE EDDINGTON CLAN

Frederick Eddington's family ties to Africa went beyond those with his father. His grandfather Jon Luc served as a palace guard for Leopold, the King of Belgium. Jon Luc volunteered to join the Belgium expeditionary forces sent to the Congo to establish a military presence for the colony in 1879. Five years later, the Europeans carved up the African continent in the scramble for Africa and gave the Congo to King Leopold. Germany and Britain had given Leopold most of the Congo Basin, a million square miles of bush and jungle. Jon Luc Eddington rose through the ranks quickly to the become commandant of the Force Publique garrison in Leopoldville. His wife joined him later.

Two generations of Eddingtons had been born in Africa, but not Frederick. His mother did not like Africa and refused to give birth in the Congo. She returned to Belgium and swore never to return to Africa. Baby Frederick arrived early on the ship headed to Belgium. His innocence would soon be replaced with a lust for power and wealth. As soon as Frederick was old enough his father brought him back to learn the family business.

Jon Luc Eddington was responsible for Uncle Jessie's trip to the States. His Force Publique garrison burned Jessie's village to make room for a rubber plantation. However, Jon Luc was secretly searching for diamonds. His spies told him of the legend of diamonds the size of eggs. Jessie's father was the village Shaman and spiritual leader. Jon Luc's spies killed Jessie's father to make him an example to the village. Eventually everyone was killed after they were tortured for information about the location of the diamonds. Jon Luc became fond of cutting off hands and feet of children to persuade the parents to talk. He collected ears as souvenirs if the torture proved to be particularly helpful in finding gold or diamonds. Otherwise, he would burn the bodies with no mementoes taken. He kept a jar of his prized ear collection in his safe as a reminder of successful persuasion. Frederick inherited Jon Luc's collection, which was his most prized possession. Like his grandfather, he liked to collect souvenirs too. Jon Luc did not leave witnesses behind to report on his private search for treasure.

Jon Luc's troops sacked Jessie's village, searched for gold and diamonds, then burned the buildings to the ground. They did not find what they were looking for. Jon Luc believed a fortune was buried under the altar in the Shaman's house, according to information he obtained from his spies. Fortunately, Jessie was visiting a mission near Leopoldville when they attacked. After learning his troops had killed everyone but the shaman's son, which happened to be Jessie. Jon Luc ordered a search for the boy. He thought the boy would know where his father hid the treasure.

A Negro preacher named Joshua Goddard from South Carolina ran a mission in the Congo supported by AME Church of Charleston. News of the massacre at Jessie's village hit Joshua hard. Jessie was his best student and Joshua knew if Jon Luc's troops were searching for him his life was in grave danger. Goddard arranged to have Jessie sent to South Carolina with several other children who were traveling with the mission choir to raise funds for Congo orphans. The number of orphans was growing steadily thanks to Jon Luc and the Belgians.

The Congo was not alone in African suffering under European colonial rule. At the turn of the 20th Century, the African continent was riddled with death and destruction under the guise of Europeans bringing civilization to the Africans. Germany, France, England, Belgium, Portugal, Spain and Italy were racing to stake their claim on a slice of Africa.

After the village massacre, Joshua knew his mission work could not succeed with the violence imposed by the Belgium occupation of the Congo. Joshua returned to South Carolina to raise Jessie as his son. Jon Luc continued to look for Jessie until he learned that the missionary Goddard might have taken the boy to the States. Jon Luc was meticulous about details he kept files on everyone including Jessie, Thomas Jet's real father and he added Goddard to his records. He suspected the missionary found out about the secret treasure and took the boy with him. Until his death, Jon Luc never forgot about

Jessie and the elusive diamonds the size of eggs that slipped out of his grasp.

Jon Luc perfected his sideline business of stealing treasure from villages in the Congo and smuggling his loot out of Africa. Over a period of forty years, he became enormously wealthy. He passed this lucrative business on to his son Peter and ultimately to Frederick. It had been rumored that Peter smuggled industrial diamonds to the Nazis during World War II. Officials of the Congo would never admit to funneling diamonds to Hitler's Germany but resourceful people like Peter and Jon Luc never let the rules stand in the way of profit.

By 1960, the family business had expanded from smuggling and official thievery to export and mineral extraction. Working for the military had its privileges for the Eddington family. Frederick had a keen interest in the hunt for lost African treasure. He hoped Dr. Oble would lead him to the source of the security leak. Instead, he led him to Thomas Jet, the missing link to the lost Mali diamonds. This became the opportunity to finish the job started by his grandfather Jon Luc.

Eddington was distracted by his other projects when he got the call to go to the states. His Zimbabwe project was his latest search for gold and treasure. His plan stumbled recently with the failed coup attempt. Eddington lost all hopes of access to the land he needed for a mineral survey. His real interest was a lead on the ancient lost treasure of Great Zimbabwe. Stymied by unexpected government interference, he devised a plan to obtain the land through deception. He planned to undermine the legitimate government and put in a friendlier, pliable government that would give him what he wanted.

Africa was changing and the European sleight of hand had lost its luster. Eddington knew the Zimbabwe government was not going to let him in. His only hope was to contaminate the area in question to enable his surrogates to get the treasure for him.

The mercenaries Eddington hired did not know they would most likely die from nerve gas contamination. Eddington provided pills to his operatives to use as an antidote for the poison gas. Unfortunately, the pills were only sugar pills. Eddington thought if the terrorist were killed, then the believability of the terrorist threat was greatly increased. He was willing to sacrifice a few hundred money hungry hired guns to convince the world that the area was contaminated. The next step was to send in his environmental firm to clean up the area and search for the treasure while they were in total control. He said to himself, "What a brilliant idea."

Eddington called his contact in Johannesburg to set the timetable of events and start the clock. He received the news that twenty people had been killed after the first release of the poison gas. He thought his grandfather Jon Luc would be proud. A few more poison releases, there would be widespread panic, and he could take control of the area for the treasure search.

CHAPTER 11
TRANSITION

Thomas was the first to stand up to speak at the opening session of the brotherhood. Simon had arranged the meeting place. No emails or text messages were sent to the brothers. Goode acted as the coordinator for his fellow travelers. Each member received a message with a series of numbers that included only GPS coordinates, along with the date and time. Like clockwork, they walked into the room on time and without mobile phones. The new location had been kept secret and all travel was routed as it had been in Maryland. The remote location consisted of four guest cottages and a central meeting room for meals and group activities in the woods outside of Charleston, South Carolina. Thomas raised his hand, bowed his head, and said, "I am not a very religious man. The last thirty days have been full of soul searching and re-evaluation. When I met Dr. Oble, I thought I knew who I was and where I was going. We all have had experiences with dreams, visions and messages. For me, the most profound change was to acknowledge my connection to Africa. In some respects, I am ashamed I did not recognize my connection before now. The visions directed me to focus my efforts to access the hidden meaning of my purpose as part of the brotherhood."

After Thomas finished his statement, the door opened and a thin man with a cane made his way down the hall, into the meeting room. He walked easily with the cane, moving through the circle of chairs where the brothers sat. He raised his cane and said, "Fufua! My brothers, I am Maalik. Your awakening was my responsibility. Brother Thomas stated what you all feel in your hearts. I am here to tell you your mission and your role in the group, according to the prophecy. You are descendants of the original seven tribes; although you come from different tribes, you share the same experience in the Americas. Some of you are descendants of former slaves, and others are not. Seven represents the number of members of the original secret society formed in the old time, some say back in the 11th century. The single purpose of the brotherhood is to protect the vision, which foretold the destruction of Black Africa, and to prepare for the rebirth of the continent. We are the Tribe of One, but most refer to us as the Brotherhood."

"There is no nationalist goal for our group. We do not take sides on disputes between African states, unless there is clear evidence of foreign interference. Seven represents the number of major kingdoms that existed in Africa when the original vision was experienced by the old king. Your experiences over the past several months and your presence here mean that you understand that you will never be the same. What I need to tell you is that there are others like you in Brazil, Columbia, Cuba, Mexico, Jamaica, Europe and homeland Africa. You may never meet your fellow travelers in these places, but I cannot say what is in your final destiny. You must know the others exist, as they know you exist as well. You are not alone. In Africa, we are organized, planning and working to fulfill the objective of a free Africa. A free Africa means free of European domination, free of foreign aid, free of despots, free of puppet governments and criminals who rule independent African countries for their own personal gain."

"Mother Africa has abundant natural resources but our people do not benefit from such bounty. Our group cannot take sides on internal conflicts in Africa; we only deal with external threats. This important point you must remember. The founders represent the major tribes of Africa and pledged not to support any tribal interest above the goal of a free Africa. We strictly enforce this pledge and you must know that punishment is severe for any member who violates this rule. In some cases, death will result, so carefully consider your actions if you work against a sovereign African state."

Maalik stood before the group with a stern and deadly serious expression on his face. To punctuate his meaning, he passed out pictures of bloody crime scenes to illustrate the death sentences given to former brotherhood members who chose a tribe over the group's mission.

The Obsidian order was responsible for enforcement. They were trained assassins. The history of the Obsidian order was as long as the

Tribe of One. Over the centuries, they perfected living in the shadows while watching over the brotherhood. They mastered the use of knives and poison with precision. Death usually came quietly, in the dark.

"We will not tolerate any profiteering within the brotherhood." Maalik raised his cane to get everyone's attention then said, "Anyone who wants out, leave now, otherwise the only way out is through death!"

The brothers glanced at each other, but no one moved. Maalik announced, "With your silence, your contract is complete. Your role is to work together to effectively achieve our goal. We do not use telecommunications infrastructure for our purposes. The CIA, IBC and NSA are listening. If you have not researched the history of how Africa got the way it is today… this will be your first assignment. We are sons and daughters of mother Africa."

"I was awakened in the same manner as you ninety years ago," Maalik continued. "Africa did not look like it does now. The European colonial powers were well entrenched in Africa and African descendants all over the world were under some form of oppression. Today you must look closely to find the strings which control you, but be not misled … the string has replaced the chain. The impact of seeking freedom is the same if you pull away from the master, he will jerk you back by the neck to keep you in line. Your prior lives were free. You did what you pleased until you stepped out of line, broke the law or moved too fast within your respective careers or economic systems. As you move forward as part of our brotherhood your freedom will be limited to how well you plan and anticipate."

Thomas at this point reached out to shake Maalik's hand. Maalik took his hand and hugged him. After their embrace Thomas asked, "Why, after all of these years were we chosen to act now?"

Maalik smiled at Thomas and then looked at the other men. He responded, "It's your turn. Destiny is not chosen. The adversaries whom your group will face are not governments but rather business interests which use intelligence and espionage to further their objectives. These individuals use organizations like the IBC for their dirty work. Military coups in Africa are in most cases the result of those who want rubber, big oil and mineral interests while demanding greater concessions than the previous government would allow."

"Your original meeting with Dr. Oble was moved because the IBC was following him. He was killed the next day after your meeting at Rock Creek Park. This is a deadly serious business. Trust no one with our secrets outside of our group."

"Today, forces are at work to continue to enslave the African continent. Who controls the oil, gold, minerals and diamonds? Ask yourself, if Africa is not free, can you be free where ever you are? The same foot is on your throat in Chicago, Birmingham or Sao Paulo. It is the same foot on the throat of the African Continent. "

"Brazil has the largest population of blacks outside of Africa, yet blacks are denied basic opportunities of education, housing and jobs. You must read and learn your history to understand where you stand."

Maalik waived his hand to his aide and moments later two men entered the room carrying a small chest. They placed the chest on the table and left the room. Maalik opened the lock on the chest, raised the top, and proceeded with a chant. He asked the group to form a circle around him. Each man took his turn to walk around the table to view the contents of gold, diamonds and other precious stones. He said, "I've read the profiles on each of you, I am confident you can take this small treasure to do what needs to be done. Be self-reliant, no government funds, foundation grants, no white papers…just do the work. Good hunting!" Maalik reached in his pocket for the little vase, he kissed it and raised it in the air then walked out of the room.

Goode told everyone to remain seated. He asked Simon to take the floor. Simon sat for a few minutes and then said, "I don't know about you but I'm fired up. I spent the last two weeks reading more about African history. Like Thomas, I thought I had arrived before Dr. Oble cornered me in the elevator of my office building. He had a way of catching you off guard. I am sorry to hear he is no longer with us. Doc did his job. He delivered the wake up call. Now we need to get up and get into action. Maalik put a fine point on what we are up against. He's left it in our hands."

Simon continued. "I propose we set up a nonprofit research group as a vehicle for our group to study, plan and implement programs to help Africa become independent and developed. If you approve my plan, the offices for our institute of African American Studies for a Better Africa (AASBA) will open next month. We will be headquartered in New York. As Maalik pointed out, we need to work out in the open but keep our group private. The AASBA will function like any other non-profit think tank except with the help of the seven of us with our special insight."

"As a child growing up in a Baptist church," Simon went on, "pastor would always say, 'God will never ask you to do more than you are able'. The New York office will have a small support staff under my supervision. This will serve as our base of operations. I funded our startup operation with two million dollars. Based on the gift provided today by Maalik, we will need no other funding for our operations; I will submit to the group a financial plan for converting these assets into investments to sustain our operations. We also have an offer to fund our operations from the D.C. law firm of Bittle, Brass & Boyd. I have not vetted the firm to determine who they are and why they offered to fund our African study group. AASBA will pay each of us a cash stipend that will give us the independence to pursue the objectives we determine. This will not be a part time job for me. I hope you can make a similar commitment. I welcome you to the AASBA. Brother

Marcus Garvey knew what we know today. It is our time to complete the work he started."

Goode said, "Simon, I'm impressed. You are a man of action. I think I can speak for the group … we look forward to our new home office in New York."

Jamal spoke up and said, "I prayed on this before I left Houston. I am from the streets. I'm not used to working on the inside, like for a real business or in an office. When I got back to Houston I knew gang banging was over, the drugs and street did not fit with what was going on with my mind. I put away some cash for my retirement. I had some extra I wanted to contribute to our new enterprise. I brought one bag from Houston with me; it weighs about fifty pounds and is full of one hundred dollars bills. I figure this case should contain about two million dollars."

"Simon since you are Mr. Wall Street," Jamal continued, "can you convert this cash into something we can use? Brothers, you can count on me to do my part. The way I look at it, we can help the African by helping ourselves here. The same powers that keep us unemployed, on drugs, doing petty crimes, and serving time in jail are the same ones that keep the despots and puppets in power in Africa. How is it that all of the world's mineral wealth, including gold and diamonds are in Africa but Africans are the poorest people in the world? What is wrong with that picture? "

Simon was almost in tears, hearing Jamal speak. He thought about Buford and Yale Street and looked over to Jamal. He motioned with his fist, touching his heart as he pointed at him and said, "Right on!"

The evening continued with commitments from the rest of the brothers addressing issues like unemployment, dropout rates and disproportionate prison population.

Luther commented, "All of this is good but we need to keep it real. We live in the U.S. the heart of capitalism in the world. Is there a conflict between what we need to do to help African Americans, Afro-Brazilians and Africa along with the objectives of the Unites States?"

Goode responded, "No, we will not do anything in conflict with our status as citizens. As the attorney in this group, it will be my charge to make sure we stay within these boundaries."

Simon spoke to Luther's concern, "We will focus on infrastructure and utilities for certain African nations. We will examine socio-economic conditions and market solutions, which will link Afro-American and Afro-Latin American to Africa to create new capital investment into African economies. Our group will pool resources to examine various governments to determine what works best. This general approach will be applied to the solutions that can be evaluated for communities here at home in the U.S. As brother Jamal pointed out, our work should start at home."

Luther waved his hand to speak again, "Okay, I got it but why did Maalik pull our chain about the IBC, CIA and others watching us."

Goode spoke up, "Luther, where have you been? This is still the U.S. The FBI and others followed and bugged W.E.B. Du Bois, Marcus Garvey, Paul Robeson, Huey Newton, Malcolm X, Martin Luther King and any other brother who spoke out on the condition of black folks anywhere. Maalik was simply telling us nothing has changed. We should remember this always and avoid the phones and email communications."

Thomas said, "Amen to that, brother, they are out there. Since we got the gift let's use it and be smart about it."

The brothers continued to discuss issues over the course of the three hours, then broke into committees to plan the next meeting.

Simon stepped outside for some fresh air. After closing the door, he noticed Maalik was standing on the porch. Simon was startled at first, then felt relieved to see Maalik had not left.

Maalik tapped his cane and said, "Walk with me." Simon followed. Maalik spoke softly but in a firm voice. "We did not wake you to create position papers and conduct studies. You have more important work to do if you find something that needs to be studied, direct this activity to the Bittle firm. They are very discreet and know how to keep secrets."

Simon stopped walking and Maalik turned around. Simon said, "You know about the Bittle offer to fund our group."

Maalik continued walking as a car drove up and parked at the edge of the meetinghouse. Maalik said, "We know everything. Your group needs to stay below the radar. Listen to Jamal and trust his insight. Use cash for all transactions. Be invisible. Be formless. If you have no form, your enemy cannot easily attack you."

"What do you mean my enemy?" Simon stopped in his tracks to listen to Maalik's answer.

Maalik said, "Be formless and keep the group small to follow the vision."

"We are not doing anything illegal, so why all of the intrigue?" Simon had a puzzled look in his eyes.

Maalik reached into his pocket to touch the little vase, then said, "That's correct. However, the twenty million Africans stolen into slavery were not doing anything illegal either, but they were enslaved and forced to spend four hundred years in bondage. Europeans sliced up Africa like a cake with no regard for the people, its history or culture. Who spoke up and said this was immoral or illegal? We are engaged in a struggle for the survival of Africa and its descendants. You must be prepared for the unknown. Be formless!"

With that, Maalik got in the waiting car and sped away into the night. Simon stood there as the rain started to pour. He was soaking wet but did not move. He was deep in thought as he watched Maalik's car drive off into the distance.

CHAPTER 12

HOMELAND

Royce sat in his office overlooking downtown Johannesburg. He was nervous and agitated. He started pacing the floor until the phone finally rang. It was Theo, a sixteen-year-old Zimbabwean informant working for the brotherhood. He said, "I have the location where the terrorists are hiding the materials for the attack."

Royce breathed a sigh of relief before sitting down. "Theo you are not a field agent. I'm pulling you off this assignment, stop taking unnecessary chances."

Theo pulled back his braids and wiped the sweat from his forehead, his heart still pounding after following his friend to meet his father. He responded, "I had to be the one to do this. This was our only chance to find the location before it is too late. It's cool. I'm invisible and they are not looking for me."

Theo hung up the phone and went to his third period high school class. Royce paced the floor and then called Henry into his office. Henry was the deputy section chief for field operations intelligence. Royce said, "We've got to get Theo out of this deal."

"Without Theo it won't work. He grew up in Zimbabwe and he is familiar with the area," replied Henry.

"This is a dangerous situation," Royce replied as he pounded the table.

Henry tossed a dart into the map of Zimbabwe and said, "Yeah, but think about how many lives we can save if we get this information."

After Henry left his office, the phone rang. Royce answered. "Jack, I was expecting your call. Where are you?"

"I am in Johannesburg near Sandton at the Safari Inn."

"Okay, I know the place I will see you this afternoon." Royce hung up. Concerned about security, he did not tell Henry about Jack's arrival.

* * * * *

Jack had not slept much since meeting with Erd. He started having strange dreams and hearing voices that woke him up in the middle of the night. He ordered another cocktail, thinking, *I don't know what Royce looks like. He could be sitting next to me at the bar. Whenever he shows up, I'll let him pay the tab.*

An hour later Royce arrived at the hotel bar. He spotted Jack right away. He went over, introduced himself, and pulled up a seat. Jack took a long sip from his drink and asked, "What do you have for me?"

Royce said, "We cannot talk here, we need to move and talk."

Jack nodded. Royce placed some money on the bar, stood and pointed toward the door. They walked out onto the street and then Royce began to talk, "Erd told me you can be trusted. She told me about your background with the CIA and military intelligence. I run field agents in the region for our group and frankly; I need your help with a project. Your expertise with chemical weapons would be extremely helpful."

Jack said nothing. His eyes squinted, then he stared at Royce, wondering, *Who is this guy and what's going on here?*

Royce broke the silence. "All of this is strange to you. I understand. Everyone in our agency was selected as I have selected you. I used to work with British intelligence service MI6. The exception is you are connected to the seven, which makes you special to the founders. The rest of us are grunts who work in the intelligence section. We work undercover and do not have an official relationship with any government other than contacts we brought with us. If you ask anyone, including myself, we all have stories that could probably rival yours concerning the first contact with the spiritual aspect of the brotherhood. However, the work we do here is where the rubber meets the road. We deal with real threats to sovereign African governments. In the current situation a Rhodesian terrorists group is trying to undermine the Zimbabwe government.

They attempted a coup a few months ago and now they are planning a poisonous gas attack."

"You guys are not on the map, at least from what I am aware. When I worked at the CIA, we did not see any independent African intelligence organizations operating in this sphere. How long have you operated in southern Africa?" said Jack.

"That's classified," responded Royce.

Jack smiled and nodded, "Okay, now that is where I live. Tell me what you need from me."

"Thanks for limiting your questions. We suspect a terrorist group is planning another attack. Officially, the government does not acknowledge the existence of the threat but unofficially they are tracking the movements of suspected sympathizers and expelling them from the country. Do you have any resources that could help?" Royce asked.

"If I asked my contacts any questions the bells would be ringing from D.C. to London." Jack reminded Royce that he was not in any position to make waves.

"As far as the CIA is concerned we do not exist. We have agents in D.C. You know in this business when you get comfortable, you get dead. You're still alive that is a good sign," Royce responded.

"Yeah, I noticed but I thought I was out of the game. I guess you never are completely out," said Jack.

"Your instincts served you well. You cannot go back. You could put your family in danger," answered Royce.

Jack shot back, "Yeah, this fact is starting to sink in. I need a clean phone."

Royce said, "You will be set up with new papers, a passport, along with cash in euro and rand. We have a safe house outside of Joberg. I am your only contact. No one on my team will know your identity. This phone is clean. Make only three calls on this phone. You will find another phone at the safe house. Use this card for Internet …if traced it will show you to be in Jamaica. Call me at this number if we need to meet. This is your car and the map to the house. Do not go back to the hotel. We will clean it. Anything found will be burned. You are off the grid."

Jack took the car keys from Royce and said, "I like the car. This is a Vantage Austin Martin, nice. You guys travel in style. You are thorough. Where can I drop you?"

Royce responded, "You know the answer."

Jack laughed, "Yeah, I figured you did not want to ride with me. Okay, let me get to work."

Royce reached over, shook Jack's hand, and said, "Welcome home."

Jack arrived at his new address, but passed by the house without stopping. He studied the cars parked on the street and drove around the block. The house had a security gate at the driveway. In the glove box of his car, he found a remote control for the gate and the garage. Jack said, "Royce thinks as I do." There was no street parking and it was secure. Perfect. On his second pass by the house, he pulled into the driveway, which opened into the garage. Jack checked for listening devices, and scanned the perimeter for security. The house was clean. Once he got inside, he looked in the refrigerator and found it stocked with food and other essentials, including beer. Jack grabbed a beer and kicked off his shoes.

After finishing his third beer, Jack opened the large envelope he found in a frozen pizza box in the freezer. Inside were two passports with new identities, cash, a 9mm automatic pistol, a flash drive and a smaller package. He tossed the other items aside, grabbed the gun, and inspected the firing pin. Once he was satisfied it would work as designed he put the clip in, pulled back the chamber to place a bullet in the loaded position and placed the gun in his waistband. He thought, *Now that we've got the important business settled let's see what else is here.* He opened the package and found a note from Erd:

> *Sorry about the pizza but we thought you would not mind the hardware instead. Everything you need is on the flash drive. Use the phone I gave you to access the data. You must leave the safe house within 24 hours. Your contact in Jamaica burned you. The IBC traced you to Johannesburg. You are not safe here … find another safe house. A cleaner will remove everything after you leave, but do your part and do not leave a trail. We will contact you. While you were sleeping, I took some of your DNA to confirm what I suspected about your ancestry. Enjoy.*

Jack smiled and thought, *I guess I'm back in the spook business, so let me get organized.*" He studied the map of the Sandton and Johannesburg area then charted his next move. He pulled out the phone book and identified where he would go.

He removed the second sheet of paper from the envelope and started reading. It was his DNA genealogy report. It rambled for a few paragraphs then stopped at 60% match for Berber and 40% for Bantu. The report had several exact matches for his DNA for ancestry in Mali, South Africa and Zimbabwe.

Jack dropped the paper and said, "What the hell. This is impossible. I've never been there before, but that is not the point is it? Okay, whatever." He opened another beer.

The next day he burned the contents of the envelope. He cleaned the house of his prints. He grabbed his backpack, the gun and left on foot, leaving the car in the garage. Two blocks away he hailed a taxi to take him to the center of the city and located a motel that took cash and asked no questions. He set up house, waiting until Royce made contact.

* * * * *

Royce walked through the lobby of the publishing house located in downtown Johannesburg. He'd spent his life working undercover. Today he wondered what his co-workers would think if they found out what he really did for a living. He pushed the button on the elevator and sped up the twenty floors to the research department. His staff of three at the publishing house was the only ones who knew his real identity. As he exited the elevator, he caught his administrative assistant's eye. He had worked with Eve for years and her facial expression told him something was wrong. He walked past her, entered his office and turned on the signal-blocking device to disrupt any electronic listening. He tested the signal, and then Henry, deputy chief of intelligence, walked into his office.

Henry said, "I picked up the paper from the news stand this morning and the weather section was cut out. This means we only have 24 hours to pull the trigger if we hope to disrupt the terrorists in Zimbabwe. My contact must be on the run if he sent this message."

"The clock started ticking on this situation once the expulsions of white farmers from Zimbabwe escalated things. Is there an update?" responded Royce.

Henry waved his hand for Royce to close the blinds and with the room darkened; he used his infrared light pen. He pointed to a location on the Zimbabwe map to indicate the areas along the border where he suspected the terrorist would infiltrate the country. He identified possible targets, which included a compound for international election observers and several government offices in the capitol.

Royce opened the blinds. He said, "We need to stay on it. Twenty-four hours is a lifetime. We have no choice but to keep Theo in the field on this one. There is too much at stake."

CHAPTER 13

CAPE VERDE

Children playing soccer ran past a faded gray stucco building. Occasionally a ball bounced over the fence but the razor wire on the top discouraged anyone from retrieving it. Security cameras monitored the soccer game and any other activity within range.

In 1975 after gaining independence from Portugal, the newly formed Cape Verde government sold that building and the accompanying compound to a secretive group. The location was suspected to be the headquarters for a covert organization. Part of the purchase included an obscure uninhabited island near Sao Vicente. The government granted the buyer diplomatic immunity and sovereign status typically given to foreign embassies. This was unusual however, in the days after the revolution and independence the normal rules did not apply. At the time, some people speculated the former Soviet Union actually secured the property but those rumors were never confirmed.

The tranquil silence ended at the compound when an unmanned aerial vehicle, a drone, circled from above before firing a missile and destroying the building, leaving a huge mound of rubble behind.

The large plume of smoke and flames could be seen for miles. Local and international news agencies initially reported the explosion as a terrorist attack.

The U.S. State Department announced hours later that the missile strike was an accident caused by a malfunctioning drone controlled by the CIA. The spokesperson blamed the error on the difficulty of fighting a worldwide war on terror.

Officials from the Cape Verde government expressed their displeasure by recalling their ambassador and calling for a UN investigation. However after it was determined the building had been vacated and no casualties reported, the story quickly faded to the back pages of world news.

At CIA headquarters in Langley the official word was that this was an accident. Some insiders suspected an intentional target. The ill-fated drone mission was listed as a classified training exercise. The director demanded an explanation as to why live ordinance was on the drone training flight. A Black Ops unit had requested a fly over the mysterious compound but no one took responsibility for firing the missile.

The after-action report indicated a software error was responsible for the command to fire the missile. With the final report filed, the official investigation ended.

The agent in charge made a call on his secure line. The man who answered said, "I heard the package was empty."

The agent responded, "Rick, who are you working for? You almost cost me my career with this drone attack. I did not authorize this mission. I had to cover up your tracks."

Rick Dodge was shocked by the news that the building was empty. He had been paid handsomely to kill those thought to be inside. Rick responded, "No worries. You will be compensated for your trouble. You gave up your career when you accepted the first envelope from me. I own you now. Don't call me again!" Rick hung up the phone, thinking he would hear from Eddington soon.

* * * * *

The location in Cape Verde was symbolic due to the island's role during the Atlantic slave trade. Most slave ships resupplied there before making the long journey to the Americas. However, the brotherhood viewed the strategic importance of the location instead of the forgotten history of slavery there. The founders required an independent location off the continent for the organization's intelligence gathering operations. This acquisition was Maalik's first official act as director of intelligence. He was proud to see the plaque installed on the compound cornerstone. It read: African Literary Historical Society (ALHS) established 1976.

At the time, the local news reported on the government's sale of the land to the ALHS as a symbol of the country's commitment to documenting the historic moments of the emergence of a new Africa. This footnote was long forgotten. The mysterious compound and its inhabitants answered to no one in Cape Verde and operated as an autonomous entity.

CHAPTER 14

CITY OF LIGHTS

It was dusk, just before the sunset. Maalik decided to walk the three blocks to his favorite café on the Champs-Elysees. The energy of Paris made him feel younger than his years. The beauty of Paris inspired Maalik to think of what a truly free Africa would be like. Stopping to catch his breath occasionally, he marveled at the architecture along the street with its cafes, shops and the clipped horse-chestnut trees. The Cape Verde missile attack was fresh on his mind. *The IBC is closing in on the brotherhood,* he thought. Luckily, Maalik had arranged to move the intelligence operations weeks before the attack.

Maalik thought about his journey when he moved to Paris after the end of the war with Germany. He had watched Europe rebuild after the war, thinking Africa had the resources to be an economic power. However, the game of chess with the IBC was taking a toll on him. Maalik slept very little since the destruction of the compound. It showed in his face, he felt he was being followed.

He stepped from the curb with his cane and walked slowly to the café. Maalik arrived at the rendezvous location, pleased that he could report to the elders that the mission given to him was well in hand. However, he was concerned that he would not live to see it through.

Darkness had fallen and the city lights were aglow. Maalik marveled at the grandeur of Paris at night as he gazed at the Arc de Triomphe while he sipped coffee in his solitude. Maalik nodded off to sleep, only to be awakened by a man with a blind fold in his hand. Maalik stood and turned around to allow the wool cloth to be placed over his eyes, and then he got into a waiting car.

The vehicle sped through the city streets for twenty minutes then drove into the country and circled back to the city. His captors transferred him to a black van and he rode for ten more minutes until the driver received a phone call to bring him in. Maalik sat patiently with his hands on his cane. His face showed no concern or displeasure. He had been there before.

Maalik was led down stairs into a tunnel for a long way until he arrived at a steel door bolted from the inside. His escort pressed the button on the key pad. A voice answered, "Leave him at the door." Maalik was left standing in the dark tunnel until the door opened and he was pulled inside.

The council of elders had met Maalik only three times since he was selected to head the European operations of the brotherhood. He usually got his instructions by messenger or coded signs left near his apartment. This meeting meant something big was in the works. Maalik was led into a room with bright lights facing him. Maalik's blindfold was removed.

His eyes strained to see behind the lights where the elders sat. Security was tight, Maalik understood if captured, and tortured he could compromise the organization. He understood the risks when he accepted his position. Maalik had never seen their faces but always remembered their voices.

"Are you well, Maalik? You can call me Isaac."

"Yes," he responded, "For a man of my age. I'm starting to feel the years in these old bones."

"Do you know why we asked you to come?"

Maalik responded, "No, but I can only guess the attack in Cape Verde must be the reason. I think the Erd situation is a sign we are close."

"We are aware of the precautions taken; you were wise to move the operations unit. Yes, Erd's recent experience going back in time is a sign that the transformation is close. Your work is far from done. The king's vision is not clear on the path. Erd should prepare for the next time-jump window. We are aware that others know the legend of the change time. The danger to you and the team has increased considerably with the Cape Verde attack," responded Issac.

"Yes, the CIA's explanation on the drone attack is a ruse, we trust no one. I know my time is short. Can Erd really travel through time as she reported?" asked Maalik.

"Erd is a traveler who can move through time. When she travels, her path is through generations before her. Her consciousness is from the current time but her physical form is that of her family member who lived in the time of her visit," responded Issac.

Maalik smiled and tapped his cane. He said, "I knew she was something special."

"Yes, the missing link to control her travel is still missing. We need Erd to arrive in Zimbabwe on an exact date," said Issac.

Maalik rubbed his knee, grimacing from pain. He said, "What are we looking for?"

Isaac said, "It is an artifact from old Zimbabwe. We have a sketch of it; you need to show it to Erd. Her mission is to find it and hide it in a specific location where we can find it today. This is the missing link of the prophecy. We believe there may be a map to the location of hidden gold reserves of old Zimbabwe. The vault was never found but rumors and myths about the lost treasure have circulated for over four hundred years."

Isaac slid a bamboo tube across the floor over to Maalik. Inside he found a cloth with a sketch of the object. He said, "This looks like a dagger."

"Yes it is, but there is more, the information we need is hidden in the handle. The white terrorists from old Rhodesia are planning a chemical weapons attack somewhere in the country. We have good intelligence that the assault is imminent. If successful, the result would be catastrophic and contaminate the site for many years. Our people are working to thwart this threat but we cannot be certain this will succeed. The IBC is tracking our progress on this search for the missing link. As soon as Erd locates the object, leave this mark at the usual contact point," responded Isaac.

Maalik was escorted to the door and out to the tunnel blindfolded. They put him in the van and drove him around in endless circles before dropping him off where they'd picked him up. Maalik took his seat at the café, ordered a cup of coffee, and sipped in deep thought. Maalik chuckled saying, "Erd is full of surprises."

* * * * *

In Johannesburg, Jack connected the flash drive to the phone to see his instructions. The video included pictures of the dagger sketch and several IBC agents who were working with the Rhodesian terrorist group, plotting to attack a peace conference in Zimbabwe. Jack's assignment was to travel into Zimbabwe, retrieve the dagger and meet with the informant to find out the location of the terrorists. He was selected for this mission because of his experience with chemical weapons. As a foreigner, he could travel as a member of the press under the guise that he was there to cover the peace conference. Jack studied the video several times and thought, *I'm too old for this stuff.*

Jack's mobile phone rang. "Jack, we cleaned the house. You should be clear for now." Jack did not say anything.

"I know what you're thinking. Why me?" said Royce.

"Well, now that you mention it. That is a good place to start. Last week I was developing condominiums for fat rich guys. Today, I am in Africa fighting terrorists. I'm not feeling this," responded Jack.

"I agree with you. Two of my agents were killed twenty-four hours ago. Our group has been compromised. Erd sent you to us as our last chance to stop this attack. This is a dangerous assignment." Royce got emotional thinking about the death of his people.

Jack said, "Yeah, you bet it is! Why did Erd tell you I could do this?"

"Erd said she would trust you with her life. She saw something in a vision. You know she has the gift," said Royce.

Jack paused, and then said, "Well, she does have that going for her for sure. How many people are at risk?"

"We think about a thousand maybe more. They are planning to use nerve gas on a peace delegation but our source says they may contaminate a school as a diversion. This is where the heavy death toll is expected. We do not know where or when, but our source is the key to finding out where the terrorists may have hidden the chemical weapons. As you know, we are not a recognized intelligence agency and have no formal contact with Zimbabwe security forces. Frankly, if we did, they would not be much help. The situation is fragile there, resources are not available."

"A thousand children…." screamed Jack, "Christ! Who are these people? What is your source?"

"Our source is a young man named Theo. He has been missing for about sixteen hours. We are worried about him, he befriended the son of one the terrorists. Theo has been sending information to us for three weeks. We are running out of time. We set a rendezvous with him for the day after tomorrow and I can only pray he shows up." Royce's voice was almost a whisper.

Jack put his gun in his waistband and started packing his bag. "I do not like this killing children stuff. I guess I need to get over to Zimbabwe to find Theo, your informant. Tell Erd next time you talk to her that she owes me a bottle of scotch if I come back. Since your folks may have a leak, I am going to burn this phone after we hang up. Go to the men's rest room at the Zebra bar in Sandton and you will find a number written on the wall in the last stall on the right. Call me when you get there and be sure to scratch out the number. Give me the location set for the meet with Theo. What about this dagger thing?"

"This is what the terrorists are after … you have to bring this back." Royce had perked up after hearing Jack was going to go.

"Wow, this is a lot of trouble for a little knife," responded Jack.

Jack terminated the call, pulled out the battery, the sim card, and crushed the phone with his heel.

He headed out the door with his backpack and map in hand.

CHAPTER 15

POINT OF NO RETURN

Thomas received a call from Goode. "Thomas. I need you to listen carefully. You cannot attend the next meeting. I just received reliable information that your life is in danger!"

Thomas said, "I understand. I made plans to get below the radar. I will contact you when I'm safe." Thomas hung up the phone. He had turned his business over to Aunt Maggie and given her keys to his house and his Mercedes.

He left at 5 o'clock in the morning. He rented a sailboat to go out the next day on Lake Michigan. He assumed they would follow him to the marina where he was scheduled to take a rental out for a half-day sail. Thomas had no plans to return. He sailed the boat to Michigan and made his way to Toronto, Canada. He left his credit cards behind and used cash for purchases to get him to Grand Cayman. Frank's passport came in handy. He had changed a lot since the family reunion.

Thomas found the gold medallion Dr. Oble gave him months ago. He thought about what the African had said that the symbol Sankofa represented.

"Return to your roots." He wore it proudly as he ventured into the unknown.

After four days of traveling, Thomas finally arrived at George Town in Cayman Island. His taxi slowly rounded the circle drive at the Sea Palace Hotel. The door attendant greeted Thomas warmly and carried his bag to the front desk. Thomas checked in under the name Tim McIntire and waited for further instructions from his old friend Jack, who had given him detailed instructions on how to clean his trail when leaving the U.S. Jack was certain the CIA would abduct Thomas or worse, kill him. Jack who still had contacts in the Caymans thought Thomas would be safe there until he could figure out the next move. The phone rang.

Thomas said, "Hey Jack, you thought of everything. I think we're even now."

Jack laughed and said, "Brother it's not over. We cannot talk. You made it out with no problem?"

"Yes," responded Thomas.

"You need to stay there for three days. Keep a low profile. I will call you when it's time to move. I will explain when I see you," said Jack.

Thomas put the phone in a safe place. He sat on the side of the bed and closed his eyes, thinking of how much his life had changed. He thought about his trip to South Carolina for the family reunion. Before then, things had not been simple. However, he'd had control of his life, or so he thought.

Thomas pulled a picture of Jessie and his father out of his wallet. They were not smiling in the photo.

Their eyes stared intently forward as if they were not in the moment. Thomas could not get used to calling Uncle Jessie his father although he knew that was the truth. His father had raised him and that was just the way it was. Jessie would always be Uncle Jessie. Thomas' mind wandered through the last three months, which seemed more like three years.

When he drifted to sleep, he heard someone speaking to him. At first, the sound was like an echo, a muffled voice saying, "Thomas, you there? Can you hear me?" Thomas jumped up and looked around the room. He opened the door but no one was there. Thomas laid down again and then the voice said, "Thomas, it's me, Goode. I have this telepathy thing working. Only one-way for now, I tried it out with a few of the brothers. Just lay back and listen. Do not contact us until you are in the clear. If you need to confirm this is me and not your scotch talking, check the news for Seattle for a Big Foot sighting reported in Tacoma Washington. This happened this morning. When you find this, you can confirm this is real. The next time I contact you, I will start with a hum. The old African said we would possess this gift. I'm the first to use it, thus far."

Thomas turned the TV on and flipped channels looking for Big Foot news but found nothing. About an hour passed flipping channels until he stopped on a cable news channel. After a commercial, the news anchor came on with a lead story "Big Foot is back!" Thomas laughed and thought, *Okay Goode. I hear you brother.* He turned off the TV and went to sleep.

The next day Thomas ventured out of his room to go to the hotel lobby bar. At first, he was thinking he would be noticed. However, after a few minutes of sitting at the bar he realized no one cared about him or who he was. After this careful study, Thomas got thirsty for a beer and ordered a Red Stripe. He'd settled into a scotch when a man sitting next to him knocked over his glass. The man was drunk and apologized profusely.

He said, "I'm drinking more than usual tonight I just found out my firm was taken over by a mega oil company and my job is gone." He ordered a round of drinks for everyone at the bar and a double for Thomas.

Thomas wiped the spilled drink off his pants and said, "No problem."

"I'm sorry, my name is Bill Martin. I am here on vacation but now I'm newly unemployed. I guess I'm retired now. I used to manage drilling operations for a small exploration company. My last assignment was three years in Africa." Thomas perked up when Bill said Africa.

"How did you like working in Africa?" Thomas inquired while sipping from his new drink.

"Great, if you don't mind sleeping on oil rigs. I spent ninety percent of my time off shore. When I went on shore the people were friendly enough but I hated to see all the poverty." Bill wiped the sweat off his forehead.

"Why do you think there was so much poverty if the country has oil wealth?" asked Thomas.

Bill ordered another drink and leaned over to whisper to Thomas, "Oil is a dirty business, thick crude gets on everything, but that's nothing compared to some of the oil deals I've seen. Most of the countries where we drill are new to the oil business. Therefore when they negotiate concessions with companies like my former employer they think after we turn over operations to the government there will be oil reserves left for the government's oil company to manage. Well, that is not the case. Let us say we have a ten-year lease with the understanding that we will develop the oil field and after ten years, the government will have reserves left to manage. Maybe this is what the contract requires but not what we do. Typically, the government never confirms how much oil we produce. We always kept a few envelopes full of cash for the inspectors who came to the rig for lunch. We drill as many holes as fast as we can to get as much oil out before the end of the lease. Oil tankers line up night and day at our rigs, making tracking how much we pump difficult. The company has no intention of leaving any oil behind." Bill finished his last drink and stumbled against the bar. He placed a wad of money on the bar.

Thomas moved out of Bill's way. He said, "You should get some sleep. You will be better in the morning." Bill waved and staggered to the elevator.

After Bill left, Thomas started a conversation with a woman sitting across the bar. He bought her a drink and asked, "Do you know of a good restaurant?"

She responded, "The Blue Sail restaurant is across the street. They have the best sea bass on the island."

He asked if she would join him for dinner. She flashed her wedding ring and said, "I'd love to, but he would object. He's out fishing today."

Thomas tipped his hat to the woman and headed across the street to the restaurant. Entering the establishment, Thomas noticed only three tables and just a bar. The menu was posted above the bar on a chalkboard. They called the customers to pick up their meal when it was ready. Thomas studied the menu, and placed his order. After and few minutes the bar keeper came back to ask Thomas for his drink order. Thomas ordered a club soda on the rocks. The bartender poured his drink and placed a slice of lime on the side. He asked, "You must have already drunk your liquor somewhere else."

Thomas smiled and said, "Yeah something like that."

The bar keeper said, "This happens a lot around here. My name is Louis. Are you from the States?"

"No, Canada. Great to meet you, Louis, they call me McIntyre. I heard the food was good here."

Louis grabbed a towel to wipe down the bar. He looked over to Thomas, set a bottle of scotch on the bar, and said, "I've been tending bar for twenty years. I'm a good judge of what folks drink. You are a scotch man. Right!"

Thomas nodded, "You know your craft." Louis raised his hand to give Thomas a high five and then walked over to ring the bell at the end of the bar.

Louis shouted, "I knew it. The next drink is on the house."

Thomas looked around the bar; no one else was in there but him and Louis. Thomas said, "Thanks, but I cannot accept a free drink. I can pay."

Louis squinted his eyes and charged up to Thomas, saying, "I own this place, and if I want to give away whisky it's my business. Therefore don't ruin my day."

Thomas smiled, "Okay, it's your money. Thank you for your hospitality."

Louis relaxed, "Now that's how you should accept a drink from a stranger. I used to live in the states. I left twenty years ago and never looked back. I cashed in my chips and my 401k, bought this place and have not regretted one day."

Thomas poured himself a drink and asked, "Why did you do it?"

The cook yelled out, "Order up!" Louis reached through the service window, produced a plate over flowing with seafood and steamed vegetables. Louis set the plate on the bar in front of Thomas. Thomas inspected the plate and said, "All of this for five dollars?"

Louis smiled, "Yeah, the owner makes his money on liquor sales, the food is extra profit."

Thomas laughed, "Okay, Louis you got me. I'm going to enjoy this meal." Thomas dug in and did not look up until Louis refilled his water glass.

As Thomas ate his meal, Louis pointed to a picture over the bar. He said, "McIntire, see this picture. This is me twenty years ago. I was an investment banker in San Francisco. I put together venture capital deals for start-ups down in the valley. You asked me why I gave it all up. Well, I will tell you. I was working a deal that would make me a lot of money that required Washington to change the rules at the FCC. After three months working with lobbyist and public relations firms, we put together a program to lobby for changes we needed. The FCC changed the rules and we went out to celebrate. Our team dined on steaks, expensive wine and drank until the wee hours in the morning. The president of the lobbying firm shared several drinks with me. After hearing his insight, I decided to make a change."

Thomas finished his meal and pushed back from the bar with a glass of scotch and a cigar graciously provided by his host. Louis told Thomas to check out the bar and asked if he saw anything missing. Thomas scanned the room and looked behind the bar, and then he said, "There are no televisions."

Louis grinned and said, "Give that man another cigar. That is right. What I learned from the lobbyist is the little known secret about the States. The country has no memory. The lobbyist explained studies conducted with focus groups on various topics and how over time, his industry had shaped and reshaped public opinion to meet their clients' objectives. He said if you control the media, including Hollywood, you control the public's ability to remember. It's like mass amnesia, people just forget the truth. They accept the media's version of reality. His final point was that most people do not read to obtain information about what is going on in the world. Yeah, they will read the sports section, tabloids, or fiction, but not history or international news. He said this void gives us an opportunity to control public opinion. This is why lobbyists are paid millions to get the rules changed in Washington."

Louis sipped his beer as he said, "I went to my hotel that night, flipped through the channels on television and thought about what the lobbyist told me. I realized living in the States was like living in a bubble. My family vacationed here in 1986. I bought this bar and never looked back."

Thomas asked, "Don't you miss your friends or just familiar places?"

Louis responded, "Yes, at first I did, but then I started to read more and here my news is not filtered. My friends can always visit."

"I never thought about that, but you've got a point. We are being bombarded with filtered news, public relations campaigns and Hollywood propaganda," replied Thomas.

Louis said, "I am unplugged and happier than I have ever been. That's why you get a great meal for five dollars."

Thomas finished his drink and announced, "Louis, I shall return. This was an excellent meal I need to walk it off down on the beach."

"Come back anytime. The dinner crowd starts at 6:00. This is when I usually duck out until closing. I hope you enjoy your stay in paradise!" responded Louis.

Thomas strolled to the corner, passing through the shopping district lined with shops selling gold jewelry and tourist trinkets for the cruise ship industry. As he walked over the ramp, down to the beach, he thought, *I wonder if I could unplug like Louis. He seems happy enough and he is right about the bubble in the States.*

He remembered how he was before the trip to Baltimore with Frank. Frank refused to plug in. His work with troubled kids and academia gave him the flexibility to think outside of the box. Thomas admired Frank's commitment to the community and for not selling out to capitalism.

Thomas called Frank before he left Chicago and encouraged him to follow up with Jamal in Houston. Frank could help Jamal make his transition from running the streets to his next phase. Although Frank was not a member of the brotherhood, he did have a part to play.

Thomas was changing. He fled the country. He did not know where he would end up except one thing was certain. Jack would not let him down. Thomas sat on the beach until the sunset and then headed back to his hotel. Louis waved and said, "Stop by tomorrow for the special."

"I will be back," said Thomas.

The next morning Thomas grabbed his backpack and went for a run on the beach. On the way back, he stopped by the marina to check on renting a boat instead of staying at the hotel. He came upon a yacht he had seen in a boating magazine in Chicago. He had placed this boat on his wish list for sailing around the world, the trip he dreamed of but knew it would never happen. The yacht had three decks, sleek lines and everything state of the art electronics including navigation, galley, fitness center, full sauna, and automatic pilot. Thomas thought, *This is an Orucoglu built in Turkey, a real beauty.* He stood staring at the boat for about ten minutes until a woman came up behind him.

She asked, "Do you sail?"

Startled, Thomas stuttered, "W...well, depends on who's asking?" He turned around to face a striking bronzed woman with hazel eyes wearing a string bikini. He was speechless.

She extended her hand and said, "I'm stranded here with this darn boat. The captain is ill… in the hospital for the next two weeks and I need to get to Belize by Saturday. Can you help me?"

Thomas caught himself staring at her breasts. He looked away, then said, "I can sail, but I am not familiar with these waters." Suddenly feeling faint, he grabbed her hand and passed out on the dock. He woke up lying on a sofa on board the yacht. The woman was leaning over him pressing a damp cloth on his forehead.

"You felt it too," she asked

Thomas said, "Felt what? I passed out."

"The link," she responded.

Thomas sat up and looked around the boat. He asked, "How did I get down here?"

She reassured him, "Calm down. I had the crew carry you aboard."

Thomas rubbed his eyes and asked, " Who are you?"

She blinked her eyes, took his hand, and placed them on her breast. She said, "I am your soul mate. My name is Oshalo Seehwo Erd but most people call me Erd."

Thomas stood straight up in shock, "How did you find me? No one knows I am here."

She grabbed him around the waist. "I am a member of the brotherhood. I sent Dr. Oble to South Carolina to meet you, remember?"

Thomas pulled away. He said, "Yes, but I had no idea you were this fine. No, I meant to say that I had a link with you."

Erd responded, "After I spoke to Jack Regis, I realized you were connected. Dr. Oble knew there was something special about you when he set up the meeting in Virginia. I could not make the meeting. If I had, things would be much different."

"You know Jack?" Thomas responded in shock.

Erd smiled and grabbed Thomas around his shoulders. "Yes. Jack is with us now. I asked him to go to Johannesburg."

Thomas said, "Slow down. I just spoke to Jack yesterday and he did not mention anything about that."

"Thomas, he could not tell you over the phone. He knows about the brotherhood. When we get to Belize, you can talk to him. Nevertheless, you are not safe here. We need to leave soon," Erd replied.

Thomas said, "How can I confirm you are who say you are?"

Erd melded her thoughts with his. He could see her with Jack and Dr. Oble. Finally, she linked his thoughts with Goode in Seattle for good measure. After this, he sat down, stunned. He said, "Okay, I got the picture. You and I are heading to Belize. Do you have any charts to map the course?"

Erd said, "Yes, the crew has already set the course and raised the anchor for the trip." Thomas said, "You were not telling me the truth about needing help to get there."

Erd rubbed his shoulders. "I could not go without you. I need you with me. Please forgive my little deception."

Thomas looked around his dream yacht and then at Erd. He sighed, "Well if I have to go, this is the way I would like it to be." He smiled, "Tell me everything I need to know." The yacht slowly sailed from port into the sunset.

CHAPTER 16
THE CONGO

Thomas woke up to the aroma of bacon and pancakes. The smell brought to mind Aunt Maggie and memories of growing up in Chicago.

Erd rolled over, kissed him on the neck, and laid her head on his chest. "Last night was wonderful … you made me scream for joy." Thomas rubbed his eyes, still groggy from the champagne, but he remembered the wild evening with Erd.

He said, "Yeah, well, it's a good thing we are in the middle of the ocean otherwise the neighbors would be complaining."

Erd sat up and smiled, then got serious, "Do you know why you are here?"

Thomas responded, "No, but I am sure you will fill me in. Government agents are following me. It has something to do with my father, Jessie and Dr. Oble."

Erd reached into her purse and pulled out her PDA then she said, "You are correct, but they are not real federal agents. These men are IBC agents. We believe they suspect you may be the missing link for finding a lost treasure. Your father, Jessie, was the last in the line of six generations of seers in his family. He moved from the Congo over one hundred and twenty years ago when the Belgian government took over his village. Jessie's father passed oral histories to him as his father did to him. He most likely passed the secret message about the treasure to you.

Within these messages is information of where centuries earlier the Mali Kingdom hid part of their royal treasury. The IBC has developed para-psychological technology capable of extracting information for the search of lost treasure from ancient African kingdoms. The US was not the only government with a remote viewer program. After the collapse of the Soviet Union, the IBC recruited psychics from the soviet program. IBC's psychics are used like bloodhounds to target our members to undermine our intelligence network. They use torture, mind control, and drugs in their data extraction process. They are responsible for the murder of hundreds of people. Africa's wealth is being stolen by these thugs."

Thomas listened carefully then said, "Is this what you want from me? Are you planning to use me like the IBC?"

Erd stood up, pointing her finger at Thomas, "Those racist neo-colonial pigs are trying to rape Africa of its' birth right. Those bastards are nothing like us. We are working to revive our continent. The brotherhood is committed to funding development and documenting our rich history. We are at war with pigs like the IBC. There is a new scramble for Africa taking place right now. The race is on for Africa's natural resources … oil, diamonds, copper and the list goes on. We do not intend to let them and their clients take from us again."

"At the turn of the 20th century Europeans had the advantage of the Maxim machine gun which could shoot six hundred rounds per minute. This gun and magazine rifles made most of Europe's battles for Africa cruelly one sided. Today the struggle for Africa is through corruption and espionage engineered by organizations like the IBC."

The ship's steward rolled in the table with breakfast and poured coffee and juice. Thomas and Erd sat quietly. Thomas reached across the table to take Erd's hand.

Erd smiled, "I was serious…you are my soul mate. When I touched your hand on the dock in St. George, I trembled and felt a deep connection with you. Tell me about your father."

"He started me on this roller coaster ride. He died when I was seven. Not much more, only that he was from the Congo," replied Thomas.

"The Congo was a dangerous place when your father left there," said Erd. With tears in her eyes and she whispered, "If the missionary Goddard had not taken your father to the States, you would not be here today. Belgium is responsible for the deaths of over 10 million people in the Congo. The Belgians stole children from their families to create the military to become soldiers not much different from what happens today in conflicts in Africa. King

Leopold ordered hands of children to be chopped off if they did not collect enough rubber to meet their family's quota of rubber production." Erd wiped the tears away from her eyes and walked out of the cabin to the deck.

Thomas followed her and said, "I was not aware why Jessie came to be in the States. That is terrible about what happened in the Congo."

Erd grabbed the rail and turned around, facing Thomas. She gazed into his eyes and said, "Our founders saw the holocaust in the Congo and all of Africa in their vision hundreds of years ago but they could not change the future, no more than we can change the past. However, with the brotherhood, we can make Africa's future brighter by recording our history for generations to come. Never again can we allow the West to dominate our continent. We must not forget the tens of millions who died."

Thomas said, "Africa is ruled by Africans today. Why not take your case directly to them?"

Erd responded, "Our focus is on external threats to Africa. We use intelligence-gathering techniques to thwart western efforts to undermine legitimate governments. The work we do is concealed from most African nation states. Unfortunately, African dictators and despots are stealing the wealth of the continent. These bad apples have no interest in the people and are no different from the Africans who sold their brothers into slavery."

"I met this guy at the hotel bar on Cayman Islands a few days ago. He had been in the oil business. He described how the oil companies were undermining African government oil reserves by over drilling leases. I couldn't believe he told me this at the bar." Thomas was shaking his head in disbelief.

"This is a notorious situation in the oil industry and mineral extraction generally; unfortunately our African brothers are allowing this to happen through corruption and ignorance. This is why we are in this fight." Erd stood up, with her fingers clasped on the back of her head.

"All this is confusing to me. Why are we going to Belize? What does this have to do with the founders or Africa?" Thomas said, pacing the floor with his hands in his pockets.

Erd smiled and winked at Thomas, "We think your great......great grandfather made this trip before Columbus discovered America."

"Wait a minute. Are you saying Africans sailed to America before Columbus?"

Erd said, "Well, yes and they made many visits too. This is why the study of African history is important for our group. We follow the trails of our ancestors to find clues about our future. My psychic gift has opened many doors, which have been closed to us for hundreds of years. The vision from the founders tells us of travel to the new world by a Mali King and his court. We think your great.... great grandfather may have been the royal shaman for the king. If this is true, your presence in Belize could help us locate the missing treasure from the voyage.

You and I are going to find his final resting place."
Thomas was astonished by Erd's announcement.

* * * * *

Thomas decided to tour the boat to clear his mind. He bumped into Zek in the galley, introduced himself, and said, "Are you part of the crew?"

"No, I'm here with Erd." Zek reached to shake Thomas's hand, and then embraced him with a hug. He said, "I know all about you. It takes a while to adjust to the brotherhood, but you will."

"Yes, I'm getting the picture. Do you live on Cayman Island?"

"No, Sao Paulo, Brazil. The brotherhood is alive and well there thanks to Erd."

"I've always wanted to go to Rio. It sounds like paradise," responded Thomas.

"Yes, the tourist industry does an excellent job promoting Carnival and the beaches. It's a great place to visit. However, for brothers and sisters who live in the cities and slums it is a daily struggle to survive." Zek turned away to open the icebox. He handed Thomas a beer while he popped the cap off his bottle.

"Like it is in the States in the inter-city, right?" asked Thomas.

"Not really, imagine what the US would be like today for blacks if the civil rights movement never happened. It's complicated brother. " Zek pulled out his wallet to show Thomas a picture of his family.

Zek finished his beer and shook Thomas' hand and continued. "There is much work to do, welcome on board. I will see you in the morning." Zek left Thomas in the Galley.

Later that evening as the sun was setting; Thomas climbed up on the rail on the front of the yacht and stared out at the horizon. The waves crashed against to the hull of the boat. The ocean spray pelted his face. He thought, *This is one hell of a family reunion.*

CHAPTER 17

LET THE WORK BEGIN!

Simon sat waiting for his contact in Switzerland to provide the status of the asset conversion for funding for the group. He paced the floor. The phone finally rang. Simon answered and the voice on the other side said, "The value of the chest and its contents converted to thirty seven million dollars. The paper currency amounted to $2.4 million. The proceeds will be deposited in offshore accounts per your instructions. Furthermore, per your instructions we invested in the specified mining operations in Ghana and Mali." Simon terminated the conversation.

He walked down the hall to the boardroom to announce the good news. Simon walked in while Goode was reporting on the status of the communications options for the brotherhood. Goode passed out a copy of the security profile of possible threats to the group and individual members. They did not disclose why Thomas was on the person of interest list. Clearly, the government was tracking the movements of Thomas. Goode collected the copies and shredded them on the spot.

Simon outlined the initiatives discussed at the meeting held in South Carolina. He said, "Maalik's visit brought into focus what needed to be done." He reminded the brothers that each member brought a different perspective to the group, which provided them with a wealth of knowledge for the program.

Jamal presented his report on intercity issues, gang violence, drugs and the risks black men faced with exposure to the judicial system. He reported that thirty percent of all African American men in Georgia and Florida have felony convictions. Jamal had not slept much over the past thirty days thinking about what the system was doing to black men. He was also concerned about security and he wanted to make sure that his two- million investment stayed under the radar. He knew the risk.

Jamal said, "We need to rethink how we run our business. Some of the brothers are used to skyscrapers, limousines, and such. We need to roll slow and not make waves that will draw attention to ourselves. Maalik said we are a secret society over nine hundred years old. The brotherhood did not survive and remain effective with a name placed on everyone's door. That old man walked into our meeting with $37 million worth of gold and diamonds. You don't do that without knowing how to be discrete. Otherwise you end up with a hole in your head and your pockets turned inside out."

"I do not think we need offices other than to be the front for our group. If we meet, we need to stay mobile. Never meet in the same place twice as a group. We should work independently or in small groups of two or three. When we need to fund a project, we should misdirect where the funds come from not to draw attention to our purpose."

"As I see it we are not drug dealers but we are more dangerous to the system because we are dealing in freedom. I've got no problem with Simon up here in the high rise because this is where he comes from, but the rest of us should find our place where we fit and work from there."

After he finished talking, Jamal pulled his 9mm automatic out his waistband and placed it on the table in front of him. Before Simon started to speak, Jamal interrupted him and said, "We will need real security for our group. This is the job I will take for the brotherhood. Does anyone object?"

Simon picked up the report prepared by Jamal and made a motion to vote on Jamal to be head of security. The vote passed unanimously.

* * * * *

Simon returned to New York with a feeling of immense pride. He had a brief case full of ideas and enough funding to make things happen. His assistant met him at the elevator with an urgent message from Buford's sister. Simon dreaded making the call.

She answered the phone, "Simon, Buford passed away last night. He was coming home from the corner market, and a drive-by shooter caught him at the red light. He died at the scene. I found your card in Buford's wallet; I thought you would want to know."

Simon paused and said, "Thank you for calling me. I would like to attend the funeral. He was my dear friend. Can I help?"

"No," she said. "Buford would not have it. He was proud. He put aside his funeral money years ago and he made me promise to follow his wishes to the letter. Your being here is all he would want."

Simon hung up and walked out to the elevator to go home. Buford's death was a reminder of why Simon made the change in his life for the brotherhood. Simon thought, *Buford took me down to Yale Street and put me back in touch with my roots.* He wondered if Buford asked him to go to the store just for that purpose.

CHAPTER 18

THE FOUNDERS

The yacht anchored in the bay outside of San Pedro, Belize. The sun was low in the sky with a strong breeze from the west. Thomas climbed the stairs up to the wheelhouse to take the helm of his dreamboat. He had almost forgotten how he got there from Chicago. Thomas was determined to live in the moment, not looking too far ahead into the future. The crew was busy preparing for a trip to shore in the morning.

Thomas wondered why the captain did not dock the yacht at the marina. He scanned the horizon until his eyes became fixed on a small island off the port side of the yacht. Thomas shouted over to Erd, "Check out the long boats. Where did they come from?" He pointed toward the bay and said, "There are hundreds more on the horizon." He started waving his hands in the air but the boats rowed past the yacht with no notice of him.

Erd walked over to him and whispered into his ear, "This is your first vision. Study and remember."

Thomas stopped waving his arms. The boats disappeared. The crew was staring at him, as if he had lost his mind. Erd motioned for Thomas to follow her to the galley. As Thomas turned the corner to catch up with her, she grabbed his hand. Erd whispered, "The African king, the founder, whose original vision started the brotherhood warned Africa to hide some of its wealth in the new world across the great water to the west. The old king described egg shaped spheres of glass that sparkled in the night or day. The founder believed these stones would be of immense value in the future and the key to Africa's freedom from foreign invaders. Two hundred years later, the Mali King Abubakari Bakr II (Abu Bakr II) ordered an expedition of two thousands ships to find the new world. The king himself led the mission."

Erd explained, "Mansa Musa succeeded Bakr II in 1312. He was reported to be the wealthiest man in the world with an estimated net worth of four hundred billion dollars if you adjust his wealth with inflation. Historians believe the Mali kingdom with its vast gold holdings was the richest in the world during this period. The Mandingo king took a historic pilgrimage to Mecca laden with gold gifts. His caravan had eighty to one hundred camels, which carried three hundred pounds each of gold equaling a total of thirty thousand pounds. In today's dollars, this would be worth over seven hundred million dollars. The legend of this massive show of wealth reached as far away as England. In hushed corridors of castles throughout Europe and Spain, there were those who plotted to find the source of the gold of Mali. It is not a coincidence the first trading post in

Africa established in 1482 was the slave fort Elmina in Ghana."

Thomas said, "That's almost a billion dollars in gold. I did not know the Africans had such wealth back then. He gave all that gold away?"

 Erd said, "Yes. If Mali had this level of wealth, King Bakr II could have easily financed his expedition to the west." Erd then pulled out her PDA and showed Thomas the following quote found on Wikipedia of Mali King Mansa Musa in 1330, as recorded by the Arab-Egyptian scholar Al-umari:

> The ruler who preceded me did not believe that it was impossible to reach the extremity of the ocean that encircles the earth (meaning the Atlantic): he wanted to reach that (end) and was determined to pursue his plan. So he equipped two hundred boats full of men, and many others full of gold, water and provisions sufficient for several years. He ordered the captain not to return until they had reached the other end of the ocean, or until he had exhausted the provisions and water. So they set out on their journey. They were absent for a long period, and, at last just one boat returned. When questioned, the captain replied: 'O Prince, we navigated for a long period, until we saw in the midst of the ocean a great river which flowing massively. My boat was the last one; others were ahead of me, and they were drowned in the great whirlpool and never came out again. I sailed back to escape this current.' But the Sultan would not believe him. He ordered two thousand

boats to be equipped for him and his men, and one thousand more for water and provisions. Then he conferred the regency on me for the term of his absence, and departed with his men, never to return nor to give a sign of life.

Thomas read the text in disbelief. He said, "Did this actually happen? Where did they go?"

"We believe they came to Belize. Belize is our Mayan connection for our search for lost Mali treasure. The Mali King relied upon scholars from Timbuktu when he planned his voyage to the Americas. A shaman who is believed to have traveled on this expedition wrote a manuscript found in Timbuktu five years ago. Included on the manuscript is a map of the coastline, similar to the characteristics of San Pedro. We believe this document came back from King Abu Bakr II's journey to America. According to legend, included in this expedition were over two hundred ships laden with jewels, diamonds and gold." Erd showed Thomas the manuscript and the shaman's map. She over laid the map with a current outline of the Belize coast where San Pedro was currently located.

Thomas studied the map and manuscript. He said, "The manuscript sketch is similar to the map of San Pedro. Nevertheless, how do you connect this map to Belize? This coastline could be anywhere else in the world with similar characteristics. Is this all you have?"

Irritated Erd explained, "In 1562 the Spanish friar Diego de Landa destroyed all of Mayan historical records which included over two million sacred images and hundreds of manuscripts. These documents could have included evidence of African influence in the development of the Mayan empire. The destruction of historical documents is a pattern of Spain's ruthless conquest in the Americas.

"But how do you know the Mali King came to America, or even Belize?" questioned Thomas.

"There is evidence that Africans came to America. We believe Landa's destructive act with Mayans records is the catalyst that prompted the Spanish role in the destruction of African historical records located in Timbuktu. The Moroccan army with Spanish mercenaries and European firearms invaded Timbuktu in 1591. The University of Sankore, which stood for over five hundred years, was destroyed. The entire Sudanese intelligentsia in Timbuktu was captured and the majority was massacred. We suspect the mercenaries were actually agents of the Spanish King directed to destroy Timbuktu as the intellectual center in Africa and capture their scholars. " Erd spoke with conviction.

"This is fantastic. You think the Spanish destroyed the Mayan records to hide the truth about Africans traveling to America first." Thomas shook his head.

"Yes, but this was part of a larger European strategy to destroy the history and intellectual institutions of West Africa. The invasion of Timbuktu was revealed in the prophecy of the founder of the brotherhood. His vision disclosed that foreigners would invade Africa and later dominate the entire continent. The first sign foretold is the destruction of Timbuktu. By 1891, three hundred years after the fall of Timbuktu, all of Africa was colonized by the Europeans except for Ethiopia."

Thomas said, "This is an extraordinary story. It's difficult to believe."

Erd stood in front of Thomas and said, "You are the missing link to this lost treasure. We think your great…great grandfather wrote this manuscript and drew this map."

"I don't know where the treasure is. I have never been to Belize." Thomas pushed the map across the table, shaking his head in disbelief.

"Did you not just observe hundreds of long boats?" Erd asked, pointing her finger at his chest.

Thomas responded, "Yes, but they vanished….."

Erd interrupted Thomas to explain, "Recently experts revealed research that confirmed Africans visited the Olmecs in America years before Christ. The Mayan pyramids are similar to those of Egypt and Nubia. There is a connection between the Mayan and the African."

She gave Thomas a picture of one of the colossal stone heads with African features, flattened nose and wide lips found in La Venta, Mexico near Belize. "Does this look like an African to you?"

Thomas glanced at the picture, "I'm no expert of what looks African."

"We are interested in the Mayans because they evolved from the Olmec civilization, dating back 800 A.D. Some experts believe the Olmecs to be of African origin from Ghana, Mali or the Mande." Erd paced the floor, while making her final argument to convince Thomas.

"Jessie was from the Mande tribe." Thomas stood up to gaze out the window toward the shore.

"I searched the last five years in Central and South America for signs of where the treasure could have been hidden. You already met Zek. He is a descendant from the Mande tribe like your father Jessie. Zek served in the Brazilian intelligence agency until he joined the brotherhood."

"Jack found me in Jamaica. My reaction to him was especially strong. He is an old soul like you. It is not a coincidence that you served together in the army. After I talked to Jack, we did some more research on your family and discovered why the IBC is interested in you. Forty years ago, two diamonds were presented for auction in New York. The stones were unusual due to their size and color; both were over three hundred carats perfect in every way. A law firm located in Washington D.C named Bittle, Brass & Boyd, represented the diamond owner." Erd poured a glass of wine and handed it Thomas.

"This law firm sends money to my Aunt Maggie," Thomas responded.

"Isn't that interesting? The anonymous owner of the diamonds is a man by the name of Joshua Goddard." Erd spoke as she scanned her PDA.

Thomas said, "Goddard! He is the missionary that adopted my father Jessie."

Erd continued to read, "Those two diamonds sold for over six million dollars forty years ago. The money went into a trust account at Bittle law firm. Goddard was killed in a burglary after the diamonds were sold."

Thomas said, "That's why Jessie was on the run."

"We believe the IBC has been looking for the source of those diamonds ever since. When Jessie disappeared and finally died, the trail went cold. There was no connection to your aunt Maggie or you. Since they did not suspect you were his son. However apparently the IBC must have figured out you were Jessie's son and that you might know the location of the lost Mali diamonds." Erd put away her PDA away and picked up her wine glass.

"That's incredible. I don't know anything." Thomas paced the floor.

"When I touched your hand on Cayman Island I felt a warm sensation. The old shaman appeared in your eyes. Trust me, when we get closer you will understand more. You just experienced a vision that you thought was real, waving at ships passing by that only you could see," Erd responded.

Thomas nodded, "Why are you focused on treasure hunting for diamonds and gold?"

Erd snapped, "These are not just any stones. These diamonds are the size of eggs. The Mali King had these stones especially prepared for this journey.

Hundreds or thousands of diamonds of this size would significantly influence the world diamond market. This treasure belongs to Africa. We must find them to protect the wealth of our ancestors. Whoever controls the diamond supply will have power over the fortune of certain parts of Africa. If we are successful with this endeavor, we could change the balance of power in diamond mining on the African continent. Just imagine thousands of diamonds the size of eggs in the control of the brotherhood."

Erd became emotional, "Don't you understand. Europeans will no longer dominate African mining interest!"

Thomas closed his eyes and said, "If this is true, this is dangerous. They will stop at nothing to keep these diamonds off the market."

Erd responded, "Yes, Europeans have killed Africans for over five hundred years for land, minerals and gold. This is nothing new, now we can change the future of Africa forever by taking the profit of diamonds out of the hands of Europeans. Remember they killed your grandfather, Jessie's father and Goddard for these diamonds. They will not stop unless we do something about it."

Thomas said," I understand now why we are taking the zodiac to San Pedro. We need to keep a low profile. Are we taking any weapons for protection?"

Erd picked up a basket from the galley. She said, "No silly, we are going for a picnic and a long walk on the beach. If we actually find something, do not worry, we are prepared for whatever comes our way." Thomas, Erd, and Zek boarded the small boat and sped into the distance, headed for San Pedro.

CHAPTER 19
MAN HUNT

Eddington's IBC agents found Jack's boat in Jamaica while another team searched Thomas' hotel room in Cayman, but the trail ran cold again. Phillip Holtz reported the status to Eddington, knowing the news would not be well received. Eddington answered the phone, "No excuses. He is close. He did not board a plane. If he is not on the island, he must be on the water. Check all the boat registries and find him!" He terminated the call. Phillip dreaded talking to him, but it had to be done.

Eddington was an avid collector of fine art and wine. He sat in his office, gazing at his latest acquisition, thinking about the strokes of the brush that created this remarkable work of art. He thought, *God directed the hands of the artist to make this masterpiece. I am an artist too. I use my creativity and talent to find treasure God meant for me to have.* He smiled and sipped wine from his glass.

His assistant knocked on the door, then entered. She said, "Sir, Fieldon from Johannesburg is on the phone. He says it's urgent."

Eddington took the phone, "What do you have for me?"

Fieldon was not intimidated by Eddington's curt manner. He ignored his bluster, waiting a few moments, and then said, "You need to pay me more money if you want my help."

Eddington responded, "I compensate you extremely well for what you do. You sit on your fat behind and give me lip service on getting good intelligence but provide nothing I can use."

"If that's how you feel about it then I will find someone else who wants to locate Jack Regis, since obviously you do not value my service," replied Fieldon.

"Where is he?" demanded Eddington.

"It's going to cost you another fifty thousand rand," said Fieldon.

"I need him alive," Eddington pounded the table. "The last one you found was half dead before we could start asking questions."

"No promises," grunted Fieldon as he blew smoke from his cigar.

"No deal! I will come personally to supervise this situation. Do nothing until I arrive." Eddington hung up the phone and sipped some more wine. He thought, *Only a master artisan could do this job right.* He saluted his painting and its artist.

Fieldon was a freelance private detective. He used to work for the South African Security Agency (SASA) before the fall of apartheid. His record of violence and torture was not well suited for the new government. Fieldon was not fond of politics. He liked money and had contacts on the street from when he used to break down doors for the government. His company provided security for mining companies and bodyguards for executives. His relationship with Eddington went back forty years, to when he worked for the military. His specialty was counter intelligence and general trouble making for African freedom fighters. The government was not aware of his connection with Eddington, then just like today. Fieldon did not exactly tell the whole story to Eddington. He had already killed two of the sources in an effort to expose Jack's whereabouts. All he had now was the safe house in Johannesburg and a cold trail. However, he knew one thing; Jack Regis was in Johannesburg and he was worth considerably more than fifty thousand rand to Eddington. That was enough to keep him looking for Jack.

* * * * *

Jack purchased an old car from a lot near his hotel. He paid cash. As he drove onto the side street, a man in a dark raincoat walked in front of his vehicle. Jack hit the breaks to avoid hitting the man. He reached in his bag for his gun. The stranger turned around, it was JB, his old boss from the CIA. He walked around the car and got in. "I hope you have insurance on this junker you almost hit me."

"What are you doing here?" Jack responded wiping sweat off his brow while putting the gun away.

JB opened his bottled water and took a drink. He said, "I'm on vacation. I am here to tour the gold mines and maybe pick up some souvenirs."

"Okay, and you just happened to stop in front of my newly purchased car," responded Jack.

"Get this thing moving, I don't want to slow you down. Besides, I would like to see the countryside. I retired last week and thought a vacation was in order."

"Cut the shit. Why are you here?" Jack demanded.

JB checked the rear view mirror and whispered, "We picked up your trail when you landed in Johannesburg. I thought you should know we confirmed who killed Herb. Those nasty folks from Belgium I told you about paid some contractors to silence Herb. We are sure they are looking for you here. They found your boat in Jamaica and most likely tracked you like we did."

"Why are they following me?" Jack turned off on a side street to determine if he was being followed.

JB said, "Well, they might just want to talk to you. However, most folks do not survive a conversation with these people. They are big on removing body parts if they don't get the right answers. We suspect they know of your connection with the Africans, who claim to use history to find lost treasure. We know you spent the night with Miss Erd. How was it?"

"I don't remember." Jack smiled at JB.

"Too bad, I wanted to hear some details. She's a fine looking woman for her age." JB pulled out a joint and lit it. He took a long drag and passed it to Jack. "You know she is in her 50's."

Jack coughed out some smoke and said, "No way. She does not look a day over thirty-five. Her body is flawless."

"Well, you remember something about your night together. Her people live longer than most. Her father lived until the age of one hundred and thirty and her mother one hundred and twenty. Amazing longevity, isn't it?" JB responded.

Jack smiled and said, "Yes amazing."

"One of the benefits of being a spook is you can carry contraband on the plane, and no one asks you any questions." JB tossed over to Jack a small bag with assorted weapons and electronic gear.

"You are crazy. Did you retire?" Jack took a drag on the joint.

"Yes, my last day is next week. I thought I would use frequent flyer miles on the company's nickel to tour the world. You know we have folks here, right?" JB took the last drag on the joint and flipped it out the window.

"Yes, I thought you would have assets here. You came all the way over here to tell me about

Herb," Jack said as he turned back on the main road to continue his route.

"No, I came to keep you from getting killed. They will not come after to you if you are in our custody." JB pulled out his gun to check the ammunition and tossed it over to Jack. "Keep this one, you may need it."

"Are you here to try to take me in?" Jack inquired.

"No, if I took you in, you would not be safe in our hands, I am not sure who you can to trust anymore, especially when it comes to Africa."

"I need to stay to see this through." Jack took JB's gun and put it in his backpack.

"See what through?" JB asked.

"If I tell you I'd have to kill you." Jack grinned, looking at JB.

"I've heard that before. Since my last day is next week, I will hang around to watch the fireworks. Herb was killed because he stumbled onto a rogue operation within the CIA. They had tapped into the secure files concerning trade negotiations using Herb's security clearance. Herb found out he was being set up to cover up the leak of this information. The money found in his car was planted to discredit him in case someone looked too closely at his death. We tracked the serial numbers to our cash used for paying contractors." JB's tone turned serious.

"Who authorized the payment?" asked Jack.

JB lit another joint and coughed. He said, "The records are restricted based on the serial numbers the money was paid two years ago to contractors in the Congo. How it got in Herb's trunk is a puzzle. Herb's family had been placed in witness protection after a disc was discovered in his safe deposit box. The best we can patch together of what happened is when Herb ran the check on Dr. Oble he found an unauthorized tap had already been placed on his phone. A surveillance team was assigned to follow the African's movements. When Herb attempted to find out who authorized the surveillance, he triggered a flag that we suspect resulted in his death. The disc contained a video from Herb he hoped would be found upon his death. In his video, he said he was being followed and his phones were tapped. He did not know whom to trust within the state department because the authorization for surveillance on Dr. Oble came from the security director's office. He could not understand why the state department would ask the CIA to do a job in the US. The day he was killed he was in route to your office to ask for your help."

Jack pulled the car over to the curb. He said, "I knew Herb was clean. What's going on? Do you know who is responsible for Herb's death?"

JB responded, "Nobody's talking. This thing is coming from places maybe as high as the Director's office. Everyone I contacted about the money and the disc has been reassigned to foreign locations. There are many new faces at Langley. The IBC has deep pockets and control the budgets of several countries. Their oil and diamond portfolio for their clients is worth over one hundred billion dollars. It's possible they bought access to the CIA to obtain the trade files under Herb's control. IBC had billions at stake if the US signed the new minerals trade deal in Southern Africa. This deal was to be the first of many. "

"What is so important about the African, Dr. Oble?" asked Jack.

"He was a psychic, like Miss Erd. He is also very dead. The DC Metro police called it a mugging, but believe me this smells a lot like Herb's death. They pulled his killers' bodies out of the Potomac last week."

Jack responded, "Is this why they are following me and Thomas?"

"Yeah, we think they suspected Thomas was involved with Dr. Oble concerning information on a failed coup attempt in Zimbabwe. Someone tried to take him out when his fight landed in DC a few months ago, remember, dreadfully sloppy work. They may suspect Herb got to you with information on the mole in our organization before he died. Who knows, but one thing is certain you are a target. By the way, did Herb tell you anything?" JB said, as he tossed his empty water bottle in the back of the car.

"This is crazy season. I don't know anything. Thomas was not involved with that kind of stuff." Jack glanced over his shoulder again to check if a car was following them.

"Bizarre, but that's all we have now. These folks are heavy handed, not much for finesse. Your request for the background check for Dr. Oble got you a ticket to join all the fun. This thing is above my pay grade. Now is a good time to retire and go fishing. Jack, you do not have any friends left at the agency. No one you can trust anyway. Pull over to the corner and let me out." JB tossed his lighter over to Jack.

JB said, "Keep the lighter. If you need to contact me push the tab on the side, and I will be able to find you. You have been out of the game for over five years. Remember you have to stay alive to win."

Jack responded, "Yeah that is what you used to tell me before every assignment."

JB responded, "Well it's still true. Dead men cannot collect the prize. Keep your head on a swivel. " JB stepped out of the car and did not look back. He walked on to the sidewalk and faded from sight in the rearview mirror.

Jack drove for the next twenty miles thinking about Thomas and wondered why the IBC was really after him. It would be five hours on highway N1 to Messina before crossing the border into Zimbabwe. Jack had plenty of time to think about the new developments shared by JB concerning his friend Herb and the adventure that lay before him.

CHAPTER 20

REUNION

The white sandy beaches in the distance reminded Thomas of snow. As Zek steered the small boat through the reef and on to the beach, Thomas thought of Chicago and what he had left behind. Departing the vessel, Erd followed behind Thomas while Zek gave them him detailed instructions for their pick up later.

On shore, Erd caught up with Thomas, grabbed his hand and asked, "Where is your mind? You seem far away."

"I'm here, but for a moment Chicago lingered in my mind, a lot has happened." Thomas picked up some seashells and tossed them into the ocean.

"Let's stay focused; we need to have our minds clear while we're here. I'm aware this has been difficult." Erd rubbed his shoulder as they walked.

"I owe it to Jessie to do my part." Thomas gazed out on the horizon. They continued until they came upon a cove where the beach ended.

Erd said, "This appears to be a good place for our picnic. Zek will bring the boat around at sunset so we have a few hours to talk and eat lunch."

"What are we looking for here? I doubt the treasure is on the beach," Thomas asked.

"I cannot answer your question. This is where my dream told me to go. I had a vision last night. We would walk until the end of the beach; the rest is up to you." Erd unloaded the basket and laid a blanket on the sand.

"Up to me? I have nothing. I'm thinking about snow in Chicago, not white sand and 100 degrees." Thomas threw up his hands and motioned to the sky.

"Sit down and chill for a minute. Be patient," Erd responded.

Thomas sat down on the blanket and ate his sandwich in silence. Erd was on her Blackberry, humming to herself. The sun started to set. Thomas noticed a figure in the distance walking up the beach toward them. At first, he thought it might be Zek, but as the man got closer, Thomas noticed the person was shorter than Zek. The stranger had what appeared to be a headdress on his head, no pants or shoes. Thomas pointed in the direction for Erd.

"He may be a shaman," Erd responded. As the man came closer, they heard him chanting. Thomas said, "This is getting weird … who is this guy?" He walked past them, not acknowledging their presence. He suddenly stopped at the cove, then went into the water and back to the beach and stopped abruptly. He turned toward the ocean, facing east with his hands up in the air. At that moment, Thomas walked over, held his hands up and joined the chant. Thomas was in a trance. After twenty minutes, the stranger turned and departed in the direction he had come, never actually speaking directly to Thomas or Erd.

Thomas stood silent for a long time, looking to the west until the sun was low in the sky. The sound of a boat in the distance got louder as Zek headed toward the beach. Finally Erd walked up behind Thomas and said, "We need to go. It will be dark soon."

Thomas did not say anything for a few minutes, and then he responded, "How did you know this would happen?"

Erd said, "I only knew where we needed to be. I can only sense bits and pieces of information. Like with your friend Jack you are the catalyst to some of the visions."

Thomas helped Erd into the boat. Zek steered the Zodiac toward the yacht. Thomas whispered to Erd, "I remember what Jessie told me years ago. It's as clear, as if he was with us on the beach. Now I realize Jessie used telepathy to transmit this information to me. As a child, I thought he told me nighttime stories I could not comprehend him sending thoughts directly to my mind. All the pieces fit together, I remember everything."

Erd held Thomas' hand. She said, "Now you can lead us to the treasure." When they reached the yacht, the crew reported several boats had been circling for the last two hours. The crew did not identify who they were. One of the mysterious boats finally pulled alongside the yacht and directed the captain to bring the yacht into port to register or leave the territorial waters of Belize.

Thomas told Erd the treasure was nearby. He pointed southeast, toward a group of islands. He said, "My vision showed me an underwater river that empties into a cave. Do we have scuba equipment?"

"Those are the Turneffe Islands." Zek pointed to the southeast.

"First, we need to move out to sea. We will make arrangements in the morning. We cannot register at the port. The IBC is most certainly looking for you and this boat," Erd responded as she busily typed on her PDA.

The yacht pulled anchor and headed out to sea, leaving San Pedro as a small dot on the horizon. Erd said to Thomas, "We must be patient and steady with our search. The treasure has been here for over seven hundred years, a few more days will not hurt our cause."

Later that night Thomas was awakened by a dream. He sat up, with sweat dripping from his forehead. The medallion Dr. Oble gave him became hot on his chest. He was trembling. In his dream, Maalik was sitting in the chair by his bed. Maalik pointed his cane at Thomas and said, "My time is over. It is your turn. Don't break the chain." Maalik then turned into dust and vanished. Thomas sat for an hour, until sunrise. He did not tell Erd about his dream but something was not right.

The next morning they spotted a fishing boat off on the horizon. Erd directed the yacht captain to sail closer to the boat. Erd, Zek and Thomas boarded the Zodiac to meet the fishing boat. The captain of the yacht sailed away, headed toward Venezuela. Thomas was sad, watching the yacht, his dreamboat, sail away. The fishing boat was Cuban, a relic from sixty years ago. The hull a rusty clay color, smoke bellowed from the engine as if any minute would be the last breath. On board, the crew was a surly lot, squinting their eyes at Thomas and Erd as they walked past them on their way to the wheelhouse to see the captain. When Thomas climbed up the last step, he was surprised to see Jamal standing next to the captain. He shook his hand and gave him a big hug.

Thomas said, "What are you doing here?"

Jamal responded, "I heard someone needed a boat. I have connections down here. I am heading up security now for our brotherhood. If there's going to be any trouble, this is where I need to be."

Erd followed Thomas up to the stairs and greeted Jamal. She said, "Dr. Oble told me all about you. He was right about you."

"The old African was a wise man. When we first met, I wanted to knock him out. May he rest in peace," responded Jamal.

Erd said, "Yes, he had a way to disarm you with his words and insight."

Jamal said, "Since I became a member of the brotherhood I believe anything is possible. I recruited the crew personally and equipped the boat. Do not let the appearance of the boat fool you. This boat is ready for action. The engine smoke is to mislead. If trouble finds us, we are ready for whatever comes our way."

Erd provided the coordinates for the Turneffe Islands. The boat captain said, "Most of those islands are dots of sand, mangrove clusters and swampy land. You will find only birds and crocodiles, but the fishing is great."

"That's why we're here." Erd winked at Thomas. The rusty fishing boat with its new passengers headed out to hunt for treasure.

Thomas had plenty of questions for Jamal about the brotherhood and wanted to know what had happened since he left the country. Erd interrupted the reunion with Jamal to give Thomas her phone. On the other end, a voice said, "Thomas, it's Jack. You are in good company."

Thomas responded, "Jack, where are you?"

"I cannot say. I am in good health and a long way from home. You are in danger from this IBC group. They searched your room at the Cayman hotel using contractors … maybe even CIA resources, to locate you. The body count is growing. Herb was killed because he stumbled onto a rogue group within the CIA. The money found in his car was planted. These CIA agents are working with the IBC to find you. You cannot go home," said Jack.

Thomas responded, "Yes. I've got the picture."

Jack said, "What do you think of Erd?"

"Memorable is all I can say," Thomas whispered.

"She must be standing nearby." Jack grinned.

"Right," Thomas responded.

"Well, she's hot. It's a little foggy but I know she has a hard body." Jack smiled, thinking about his time with Erd.

Thomas said, "Yelp, we got something else in common."

Erd took the phone back. She said, "Jack, I'm depending on you to help Royce retrieve the item."

"I'm on it." Jack hung up as he crossed the border into Zimbabwe.

Jamal and Thomas headed below to the galley. Erd stayed up top with the captain. Thomas had many questions for Jamal, however he could not ask until they had complete privacy. Once below deck away from the crew, Thomas said, "Jamal, this is such a surprise. I thought I would never see any of our brothers again."

"We kept you in our thoughts. Goode has perfected his telepathic ability and kept in contact with Erd since your departure from the States. Maalik was kidnapped a few days ago in Paris," Jamal said as he started cleaning his gun.

Thomas sat expressionless. Jamal pointed at Thomas. He said, "They are after you. A dismembered body surfaced near where Maalik lived. However, without the head or hands the body could not be identified. We suspect this is Maalik. The burns and broken bones indicated this person endured terrible pain. The local police are calling the crime a random murder by gypsies. There are no suspects yet. We have to assume the worst and hope for the best."

Thomas leaned over to Jamal and whispered in his ear, "Do you trust the men you brought with you on this trip?"

Jamal said, "Well, let me answer your question like this. I trust no one but you, Erd and brother Zek. The men will be fine because I pay them well and I got something they want."

Thomas said, "What's that?"

"You don't want to know," responded Jamal.

"Okay, I know you got this. We are headed to find lost treasure that could be worth a fortune," said Thomas.

Jamal said, "Yeah, I figured it would be something like that. We got scuba gear and heavy equipment to haul up the stuff. Do not worry about security we are prepared. The boat and crew will get us there and secure the area. This fishing boat will keep the locals off our backs while we locate the treasure. You know Erd is all over this, right."

Thomas said, "Yeah, well then I guess she planned this with you." Jamal just looked at Thomas and nodded.

Erd entered the galley and Thomas asked, "Why didn't you tell me about Maalik?"

Erd did not respond. Instead, she started talking about the last time she saw Maalik. She said, "Maalik knew his time was running out and he told me as much. He started carrying the ancient vase with him everywhere. Maalik said now was the time for everyone to work to do his or her part. I thought he was telling me good-bye at that time. We are getting extremely close to our objective and we must stay focused. Maalik would want us to finish what we started."

Thomas said, "Maalik appeared in my dream last night. He told me not to break the chain. Maybe it really was him, it felt real."

Jamal placed his gun on the table. He grunted, "We will finish what Maalik started and keep the chain strong."

Erd stood up, "Enough talk of Maalik. We will be there soon. We need to prepare for the search."

The three stood, embraced, and then went about readying the crew for the treasure hunt.

CHAPTER 21

GREAT ZIMBABWE

Jack's car struggled over the pothole-filled roads in Zimbabwe. The map and directions provided by Royce helped him avoid government checkpoints near Beitbridge on the Zimbabwe border. He finally arrived at the agreed upon rendezvous point for the meeting with Theo.

According to Royce, Theo was sixteen years old. He had befriended the son of one of the terrorists involved with the poisonous gas attack. Theo overheard the young man talking to his father and figured out they were planning the assault. Royce's agent in Zimbabwe recruited Theo to work as an informant.

Jack parked the car in the brush off the main road and covered the car with an old tarp he'd found in the trunk. He proceeded to the village transit station where Theo agreed to meet. Jack wandered through the shops of the town, buying a few craft items and filled his backpack with water and food in case he needed to make a move on foot without his car.

Jack had grown a thick beard and his tan had darkened from being on his sailboat the week earlier.

He hoped his appearance would help him blend into the background and not draw unwanted attention to his presence. He sat on a bench next to the coke machine with his hat pulled down over his eyes, as if he had not a care in the world. After a few hours, he actually fell asleep. People at the transit station, coming and going on various minibuses, paid no attention to Jack in his rumpled jacket and backpack on the bench.

Jack started to snore. A hand reached to touch his shoulder and shook him. The voice said, "Mister, this is the last bus for the day."

Jack jumped up, startled and said, "Alright, alright…" He rubbed his eyes and sat up. The boy who woke him up was wearing a green cap. Jack said, "Are you Theo?"

The boy responded, "Who are you?"

Jack said, "I am here to meet you." Jack gave him the phone number Theo used to call Royce to confirm his identity.

Theo said, "Meet me at the cross roads at the edge of town." The young man boarded the minibus.

Jack gathered his backpack, stretched, and continued his stroll through the town. His years of training reminded him to blend in he must keep his pacing casual and acting unconcerned to avoid being a target. After about an hour of lingering, he made his way to the designated rendezvous.

At the crossroads, Theo was waiting with his green cap and backpack. He said to Jack, "Are you a secret agent?"

Out of breath, Jack staggered over to Theo and sat on a log by the road he smiled and said, "No, I am just a journalist helping a friend. You cannot believe everything you see in the movies. Royce asked me to meet you. This is a dangerous situation for you. Tell me where your friend's father stores the materials. I will take it from there."

Theo shook his head. "I have to show you. You will never find the location on your own. We are running out of time. My friend has already left the country. His father moved the boxes twice in the last week."

Jack said, "Okay, but let's get one thing straight. When I say go. You must go. This situation can turn dangerous quickly."

Theo responded, "I understand. This is my country. These men are trying to destroy everything. I should do my part." Theo's eyes were intense. He understood exactly what was at stake.

Jack said, "Okay, we understand each other, let's go find the bad guys."

Jack and Theo walked to his car and together they bounced over rough roads for the next twenty miles. Theo warmed up to Jack as they drove along. He pointed out his birthplace and his first schoolhouse. After they arrived at the abandoned mine, Jack parked the car behind a pile of discarded shipping containers and surveyed the area. Theo showed him where the men had taken the green wooden boxes and canisters a few days earlier. Jack decided to wait until dark to check out the mine to locate the hidden materials. As they waited for darkness, Jack pulled out bottled water and dried beef jerky he purchased at the village. He and Theo ate and talked about soccer and football, until Jack's phone rang. He answered.

Erd said, "Jack, where are you?"

"I'm where Royce sent me," responded Jack.

She said, "I need you to go to the ruins of Great Zimbabwe now!"

"What! I need to finish up here," responded Jack.

Erd started crying, "Jack. It happened again, like in Jamaica. This time I knew where I was, and I stayed longer. I need you to go now! Please go now!"

"It's getting dark, I cannot find my way at night," Jack's voice was filled with doubt.

Erd urged, "The boy can show you. Go now Jack!"

Jack said in a firm voice, "Calm down. Let me ask if he knows how to get there."

Jack asked Theo about the ruins of the Castle and how to get there. Theo said, "Yes, it's ninety kilometers from here if we take a short cut over the mountain."

Jack got back on the phone to Erd, "We can be there in an hour. I will call you when we arrive."

Erd said, "Hurry before it's too late."

Jack hung up, puzzled by Erd. She sounded frantic. He thought, *What am I doing in the middle of*

Africa chasing terrorists and ghosts with a sixteen-year-old boy?

He glanced over to Theo. He was eating his beef jerky while directing the way over the mountain. Jack drove as fast as possible, without crashing over the edge. Theo was incredibly calm and not at all fazed by the abrupt change in plans or the treacherous trip over the mountain at night. Jack settled into his drive and focused on Theo's directions. He kept thinking about the nerve gas they left behind in the mine.

When they rounded the curve, Jack got the first glimpse of Great Zimbabwe. He had read about the ruins, but he had never seen pictures or anything. It was a huge structure with thick walls and towers. Jack thought, *What is this castle doing in Africa? Amazing!*

Theo said, "Wonderful isn't it? There is a mystery of who built it or where they went. I have been here many times. I dream of living hundreds of years ago when this place was alive."

Jack said, "Well, you're not the only one who dreams of this place."

The phone rang, "Jack, are you there yet?"

Jack responded, "We just arrived."

Erd said, "Hurry. Go to the tower, climb to the 14th step, and then check the bottom step on the curved wall. Find a ledge with a broken piece of granite with a mark like an asterisk etched into the stone. Pull the piece out and reach behind the rock for the object. Hurry! Please hurry!"

Jack responded, "Hold on. We got this." Jack pulled his flashlight out of his backpack. He and Theo went searching for the tower. Theo became the tour guide. He recited the history of Great Zimbabwe, built over one thousand years ago by a king with much wisdom. Theo proudly announced, "This is the largest stone structure in sub-Saharan Africa."

He directed Jack to the Tower and counted the steps to find the broken granite. The mark Erd described was missing. Many pieces of granite had been broken off over the years and taken away. Theo and Jack removed several stones but did not find the compartment with the object. Jack was about to give up when Theo discovered the ground had covered up the first four steps. He recounted and located a loose stone in the wall. Theo used Jack's knife to pry away the last piece of the stone. Jack reached into the cavity and found nothing.

Jack checked Theo's hands. He said, "Yours are smaller than mine. You try." He hoisted up Theo on his shoulders up to the opening. At first, he found nothing but decayed cloth and fragments of leather. Then he felt the object. Jack gave Theo a stick to move the item within reach. Finally, Theo had the item in his hand. It was a dagger wrapped in a leather pouch.

Jack and Theo celebrated finding the elusive object and made their way back to the car. Jack called Erd. "Mission accomplished."

Erd still in tears said, "Jack, you must bring it to me. Protect it with your life. The future of Africa depends on protecting the dagger."

"Don't worry however right now I have other fish to fry. I've got to get back to the mine to deal with the terrorist threat."

Erd said, "The IBC killed Maalik for the dagger. They know you are looking for it. Bring the boy with you, as he is in danger too!"

Jack hung up. He asked Theo, "Can you get us back to the mine tonight?"

"No problem, but it would be better if I drove," said Theo.

Jack said, "You can drive?"

Insulted, Theo looked at Jack and said, "I've been driving since I was twelve, when my feet could reach the pedals. I will be seventeen next month."

Jack said, "You've done well so far. I guess you can drive. Your parents aren't worried about you being out late at night?"

"My parents died in 2000 in a train accident. I live in a boarding school where I met the boy whose father is a terrorist. He's been at my school since his mother moved to England," responded Theo.

Jack did not say anything for a while. Theo drove the car around narrow curvy roads over the mountain. His mind focused on the mission at hand. Jack thought Theo was mature for his age. Theo had been through a lot in his short life. He was fighting for his country, no different from any young man in America.

They finally arrived at the mine. Theo turned off the headlights and coasted to the place where they hid the car earlier. They had company. Jack spotted two men walking around the perimeter, carrying automatic weapons. Theo waited in the car as Jack crawled on the ground to get a closer look at the situation.

Jack carried with him some of those electronic devices JB left with him in Johannesburg. He put on the night vision goggles. Jack picked up thermal images of six figures inside and three around the perimeter. Using the chemical agent detector device equipped with nano sensors, he detected small traces of chemical agents. Traces of sarin gas were located near the trunk of one of the terrorist's vehicles.

Sarin gas was invisible, odorless and five hundred times deadlier than cyanide. Jack remembered the sarin gas attack in the Japan subway in 1995 that killed twelve people years earlier. He spotted gas canisters he had seen before at a NATO base in Germany. He started sweating, thinking about the deadly gas.

Jack needed help for this situation. He was curious why JB had provided him with these high-tech toys. *JB did not tell me everything*, he thought. He managed to get back to the car undetected.

Theo said, "When do we go in?"

"We need to wait here and watch their activities. They are in positions that are easy to defend. By the way, we were never planning to go in. Our mission is to determine the threat and type of chemical involved. Just sit and finished your meal. I will call this in," responded Jack.

Jack drew up a sketch of the area and the location of the weapons. He identified casings for rockets capable of remote control delivery of the nerve gas and calculated the rocket range to be less than one hundred miles. Jack remembered the boarding school as the potential target. He was disturbed to discover gas canisters and rockets made in the U.S. *This situation smells bad,* he thought. Jack called Royce to report his findings and the location of the site.

Royce asked Jack, "Do you have any friends left at the CIA?"

Jack said, "No, this is not an option. The ordinance could have come from a NATO base in Europe. We have some bad apples. I have one contact I can trust but he is an unofficial contact. We need to use your resources to neutralize the situation."

"I have a contact in South African intelligence that can assist us. I need you to coordinate on the ground. Expect some company in a few hours," said Royce.

Jack went back to get a closer look to update his sketch of the mine site. He spotted two men on the hill over the mine opening assembling a rocket launcher stand. Jack needed to act before help arrived.

He called Royce, "Hey, we need help sooner than later …they will be able to launch within the hour. I will start the party. Your guys need to come in hot when they get here."

Jack went back to the car and pulled out the bag JB left him and took inventory. As he organized the contents, Theo walked up then said, "It looks like we are getting ready to go in."

"No, but we are going to make some trouble for those guys until help gets here," said Jack.

"Just tell me what to do. I am a pretty good shot with a rifle," said Theo.

"We have this mini machine gun. Do you think you can fire this thing without killing us in the process?"

Theo said, "You don't know about me yet, but you will find out. I can do anything I set my mind to. If it fires straight, I can handle it."

Jack chuckled, "I'm getting the picture of you, little Rambo." He proceeded to show Theo how to use the gun and they set up a plan to make the terrorists think their number was greater than just the two of them, to buy time for Royce. Jack had three grenades and three clips for the sub-machine gun, 9mm and JB's 45 automatic.

When their plan was set, he called Royce, "We are going to attack to delay the rocket launch. Rambo Theo and I will hold them until the South African forces can get here."

Royce said, "Theo is still with you?"

"Yeah, he is a tough little warrior. He'll be fine," responded Jack.

"I am coming with SA special forces we will be there in an hour. Hold them!" said Royce.

Jack and Theo separated. Jack threw two grenades to get their attention. Theo fired his machine gun, moving his position every few minutes, while Jack ran to the other side of the mine to take out the rocket launcher. Thirty minutes into the battle, two of the terrorists lay dead at the entrance. The others retreated into the mine, firing a steady stream of bullets at Theo's position. Jack captured one of the terrorists and disabled the rocket launcher.

Theo was down to his last clip of ammo. The leader of the terrorist group was pushing out of the mine, firing tracer rounds toward Theo's position. When Theo emptied his last clip, he retreated to the car for the last stand. Jack set up a remote control for explosives, if the terrorist rushed them. As Theo was about the turn the trigger on the last defense, helicopters appeared overhead with bright lights and commandos descended over the mine entrance.

Within minutes, South African security forces overwhelmed the terrorists. The remaining suspects were killed or captured. Jack ran to the car, worried about Theo and thinking the worst. Theo was standing with the explosive control button in his hand and beef jerky in his mouth.

Theo said, "I had saved the last piece of beef for you but when I did not see you."

"You can have it. I will buy you all the jerky you can eat." Jack hugged Theo and said, "We got some traveling to do."

Jack reached into his backpack to check the dagger. He thought, *Erd would never forgive me if I lost this thing.* Jack and Theo flew back to Johannesburg with Royce. Jack found the lighter JB gave him and pressed the button. JB would turn up soon enough.

* * * * *

Eddington's plane had been on the ground for only a few minutes when he learned of the failed terrorist attack in Zimbabwe. If anyone talked the tracks may lead to the IBC. He was furious on the phone shouting at his field agent in Zimbabwe threatening to kill him if he did not find Jack Regis and eliminate the captured terrorist.

He called Fieldon next. He was polite and greeted him, "My friend. I'm in Johannesburg. I would like to meet with you to discuss your lead on Jack Regis. I think we can come to terms on a price."

Fieldon listened to Eddington on his speakerphone he turned up the volume. He said, "I enjoy listening to you beg Eddington. Everyone is aware of the failed terrorist attack in Zimbabwe. The South African special investigation unit, the Scorpions will be coming for you soon. You should not stray too far from your plane. The South African government does not coddle terrorist and outside agitators. I might turn you in myself."

Eddington was surprised Fieldon heard about the raid. Fieldon was right. He will be arrested if the Scorpions connected him to the Zimbabwe nerve gas attack. Eddington's picture in handcuffs would be in the London Times in the morning.

"I will pay you 250,000 rand for Jack Regis. Don't worry about the SASA," responded Eddington.

"No way. This is too hot now. I could go to jail, too," shouted Fieldon.

Eddington responded, "How much!"

"One million rand dead or alive for Jack Regis. I cannot promise to deliver him alive," said Fieldon.

"I do not need him alive. I require positive identification from his body. The money will not be paid unless you recover a dagger in his possession. Get me the dagger within 48 hours and there is another one million Rand for you as a bonus. If I hear about this offer to you from anyone expect an equal bounty on your head too," said Eddington.

Fieldon knew he meant it. The money was nothing to Eddington but revenge was his trademark. Fieldon had never crossed him. He had seen the bodies of others that had. Fieldon responded, "If I find something of interest I will contact you. Watch out for flashing lights they may be coming after you." He terminated the call.

Fieldon immediately started working his government contacts to find Jack. He intended to collect the 2,000,000-rand prize for his trouble.

Eddington knew if Jack had the dagger, he would not stay in the country long. Frustrated he threw his phone to the floor. He thought, *He got to the dagger before me. How did they find out about the gas attack?* Eddington looked in the mirror. He thought, *I must be slipping.*

His assistant interrupted his gaze with a question. "Sir, are you ready for the car?"

Eddington looked at her with disgust. He said, "Did I ask for the car? Tell the pilot to prepare to leave for New York at once. " His tone was enough for her not to look at him but to back away quietly and leave the room. Eddington paid well but his violent temper is legend among his staff.

His last assistant suffered a broken collarbone for being too slow to move out of the way of his fist. She apologized for her slowness and drove herself to the hospital. He paid her well. She never worked for him again.

CHAPTER 22

TOO MUCH WATER TO DRINK

The boat circled the islands for a day. Thomas studied the shoreline to locate the place to start the search for the treasure from his vision. Finally, as the sunset he spotted the site near an inlet lagoon. The water is clear and blue like a picture post card of the Caribbean. Thomas leaned over the rail of the boat thinking about the dive they would be making in the morning. He had taken diving lessons before and received his certification while on vacation in Aruba ten years earlier.

Jamal spent the afternoon giving Thomas a refresher course on the proper breathing techniques, instrumentation and communications gear. This would be different from his recreation dives looking for fish and coral on the ocean floor. His nerves had gotten the best of him. His stomach fluttered and he threw up breakfast feeling uneasy about diving for underwater treasure. *This is a job for professional divers*, he thought pacing the deck.

Thomas was daydreaming about Chicago when Jamal shouted over to him, "Yo bro it's time to lock and load. Let's do this."

Thomas grimaced remembering his first dive. He swallowed so much water he thought there would be none left for his dive. He stayed sick for two days before he returned to the water. Jamal had his wet suit on and handed Thomas his tank. Then in an instant together they flipped backward into the ocean. Erd and Zek stayed on the boat to monitor the crew.

Jamal prepared for this dive for weeks after Maalik alerted Goode the brothers needed to prepare for underwater savage. Jamal volunteered and took on the task with an intense focus. Training as a Navy Seal made him well suited for this mission. He trained several weeks to become dive certified for one hundred feet. Jamal was still embittered from how the Navy forced him out. He is determined to prove to himself. He was ready then and now when it counts. The brothers were not aware of what happened to Jamal in the Navy. They knew he had a chip on his shoulder. Everyone steered clear of him when he got that look in his eyes. He would let you know to get out of his way.

The men floated below the boat and drifted toward the reef. Thomas marveled at the underwater beauty his mind wondered between two worlds. Jamal pointed downward with his hand. Thomas spotted the cave. Jamal led with his spear gun to investigate. They entered the opening to the cavern.

A bluish green fourteen-foot tiger shark greeted them with his mouth-opened ready for a meal. The huge six hundred-pound creature charged at Jamal and pushed him back. The beast was protecting the cave. Jamal stood his ground and stared directly into the cold eyes of the killer shark. The shark broke off the attack and let them to proceed into the cave. They searched for thirty minutes. It was a dead end.

This was nothing like Thomas' vision. Air in their tanks ran low with little time left to explore. Thomas questioned if his vision was real. They returned to the boat empty handed.

Erd was the first to greet Thomas. She grabbed his head and stared into his eyes. "Focus and remember that Jessie, Maalik and generations before you will guide you. Open your mind and find the way," she said.

Thomas said nothing. He took off his empty tank grabbed a fresh one and jumped back into the water. Jamal followed right behind him. This time Thomas led the way. He went straight down passed the earlier cave and through the weeds along the bottom. He swam into the reef forging as if looking for a place to cross a river. Thomas started searching for the underwater river revealed in his vision. Jamal had difficulty keeping up with Thomas. He kept moving in and out of the reeds drifting up and down until he disappeared. Jamal returned to the boat he was out of air.

Thomas is missing. He did not respond to his radio, nothing ...no Thomas, no diamonds. Frantic Erd paced the deck while Jamal prepared to go back in the water to look for Thomas. Thirty minutes had passed. His body had not surfaced but the sharks would have easily disposed of him.

Erd urged Jamal, "Hurry Thomas may be trapped and out of air. Hurry, hurry save him!"

Jamal motioned for her to chill then jumped into the water. He started his search where he'd lost Thomas. He went back to the reeds by the reef a current brush against his face. Jamal concentrated on Thomas then he heard Thomas talking to him through his thoughts. "Follow the river."

Jamal swam with the current into a tunnel under the reef. He was scared he would not have enough air to get back. Operating on faith alone searching for Thomas, he followed a mind link that could cost him his life. Jamal swam on until a light appeared in the distance too late to turn around. He followed the light until he came up into an underground cave. Jamal gasping for air his tank was almost empty. He knew he needed to save the spare tank for Thomas and their return to the boat. Jamal wrestled off his tanks and stumbled around the cavern looking for Thomas.

He turned the corner and discovered the source of the light reflecting off chests of gold coins. Next to the chest sat Thomas with his head in his hands. In front of him were baskets of diamonds and gold. The thin beam of light from the ceiling found its way into the cave and reflected off the gold, and diamonds, which created a mesmerizing glow that overwhelmed Thomas. He was captivated by what he found in the cave.

"Wow, this treasure is enough to change the course of the development of the continent. We've come a long way from Rock Creek Park with Dr.

Oble presiding over our induction into the brotherhood. Remember when he said 'Fufua' to us gathered around the fire. What did he say… awaken? Well, I'm wide awake now." Jamal said as he picked up some gold coins.

"My grandfather and father died to keep this secret safe. We have a great responsibility." Thomas said, he raised his head and nodded.

"We need to figure out how to get this stuff out. The radio does not work. The walls must be covered with something which interferes with our signal." Jamal responded.

"I was out of air by the time I noticed the light I just held my breath and swam as fast as possible."

Erd sensed they were safe even though she could not could not communicate with them over the radio. The cave walls blocked her from using her telepathic power but she sensed they were alive. Death was dreadfully familiar to her. The instant Maalik died. She knew. If Jamal and Thomas were killed, she would be aware of their demise. It was dark now. Nothing could be done until morning. Jamal pulled his survival kit from his pouch. He emptied the contents on to the floor he called out matches, lighter, water, flares, and one protein bar. He split the bar with Thomas for dinner. After the meal, Thomas lit the flare and tossed it up to the highest ledge. This additional light gave them a more complete view of the contents in the cavern.

Jamal shouted, "We need a bigger boat."

"Yelp, we should reconsider the original plan," Thomas nodded. They spent the night counting baskets and bundles of diamonds. The gold was easier with only a few chests scattered thirteen in all. They stopped when the flare burned out. Jamal's count was seventy-eight and Thomas had sixty-four. Exhausted they made a pillow out of several bundles of diamonds and went to sleep.

* * * * *

Morning brought trouble for Erd. Three boats from the harbor were circling. This time police and military uniforms were visible in two of the boats. Erd knew this was not a coincidence. Maalik's death and the gas attack in Zimbabwe were connected. Erd sensed the IBC was closing in. The fishing boat would agree to register with the Harbormaster for a three day fishing trip in the bay and cove area. She went below Zek and the captain dealt with the authorities. Erd hoped the Cuban registered boat would be enough to throw the IBC off their trail.

Sunrise in the cave bought a new discovery for Jamal and Thomas. The light through the crack in the ceiling moved around the walls to show more of the hidden treasure. Jamal was the first to discover it. Initially he thought this was just a shadow until he saw the eyes looking back at him. He grabbed his spear gun and went closer. The eyes seemed to follow him. As the sun rose higher in the sky, the light in the cave revealed the answer to the mystery. The eyes belonged to the king. His image was painted on the wall. Majestically he sat on a throne with his scepter robed in silk and gold. The king's eyes were so intense that wherever Jamal moved he felt his eyes following him. Jamal was standing in front of the Mandingo King when Thomas woke up. Thomas called over to Jamal but he did not answer.

Finally, Thomas walked over to check out what Jamal was looking at. Thomas said, "There is no doubt whose wealth this is. The king's image is here to protect the treasure. Jamal, the scepter resembles the one Dr. Oble gave Goode."

At that moment, Thomas felt like he had been here before. The excitement and confusion of the journey to the cave had subsided. The image of the king brought on a feeling of déjà vu over him. The feeling was very strong then faded.

Jamal studied the king's face and the scepter. He said, "I think you're right."

"He sort of favors Goode if you check out his nose and ears." Thomas agreed. They looked at each other and said, "No way impossible."

"It's eerie to see him like this. He is ruling over his kingdom down here. This is giving me the willies." Jamal slowly walked to the left to determine if the king's eyes followed him.

Thomas pushed Jamal away from the image saying, "Brother let's get back to work he not going anywhere we've got to get back to the boat."

Jamal walked away staring back at the king. He said, "You're right but he just keeps watching me."

Jamal and Thomas continued their inventory making the final count of bundles and baskets to total four hundred and seventy two. Each basket contained seventy to eighty diamonds and the bundles had fifty or less. Jamal entered the count in his notebook.

Thomas blew out his breath. He said, "This must be worth billions of dollars."

Jamal nodded and began searching for another way out. Thomas focused on the opening in the ceiling that let the glint of light. The ceiling was at least one hundred feet to the top, impossible. Jamal said," The treasure was stored here seven hundred years ago. The cave entrance must be guarded naturally to trust such a vast fortune to remain unguarded. The sea level must have been lower when this cavern was discovered. The ocean route must be the only way in."

"Let's select a few samples of the diamonds and gold to take with us and return to the boat. We can share the spare tank through the tunnel back to open water up to the surface," responded Thomas.

They agreed and packed up to leave. Thomas selected two stones and secured them in the survival pouch. He took one last look at the cave then descended into the water. On the surface Jamal radioed their position.

The boat was arriving from the harbor. Zek went ahead with the zodiac to recover them from the water. Erd was relieved to see Thomas and Jamal back on the boat. After a brief conference, they raised anchor and sailed to Honduras to regroup on how to retrieve the treasure.

* * * * *

The helicopter ride to Johannesburg was a treat for Theo. He had never flown before. Theo marveled at the ease the craft maneuvered over the rolling hills and landed on top of the parking garage. Jack ignored the flight. He studied Royce's face and the SASA officer who provided the ride. He sensed something was not right. Subdued Royce said little other than small talk about the terrain. He thanked Theo for helping disrupt the terrorist attack but was uncomfortable with comments to Jack in front of the SASA official.

Jack understood his CIA background would not play well here. Royce was careful to say little of how Jack fit into the puzzle. The helicopter let Jack, Theo and Royce off on top of the parking garage in Sandton then took off leaving them to find their way.

Officially, Royce was a publisher of an international travel magazine he called in a huge favor to persuade the SASA to cross the Zimbabwe border to engage the terrorist. There would be ramifications from the night action but all parties will agree to accept the good result without filing a report on who participated. Royce cut that deal with his government contact.

Royce pulled Jack aside while Theo walked around on the roof looking at the bright lights of Johannesburg and Mandela Square. Royce walking with Jack pointed over to the mall then said, "Look at all of this development. This is a tale of two cities five kilometers from here is Alexandria where people live in shacks with no running water. There are many contradictions in Africa even here."

"Yes, I noticed the area when we made our approach into the City. I'm a developer, so I get it. Location is everything. We have blighted areas in DC not five blocks from the White House," responded Jack.

"Mining interests still control South Africa's wealth. This will not change overnight. Jack, you saved hundreds of lives tonight. Thank you for sticking with the job to see it through."

Jack responded, "When you are on the ground you have to act based on the situation. I am getting too old for this work. This is why I retired."

"You can't retire from this business. You either live or die. Enemies never forget. I have some news for you. There is a bounty of 50,000 rand on your head here. The word on the street is you are a drug smuggler who stole some product," said Royce.

Jack laughed and said, "That's original. Who is looking for me now?"

"His name is Fieldon. He is a security contractor with ties to the SASA. His men have been passing out your picture and searching hotels for you since you left for Zimbabwe. I suspect these people are responsible for the death of two of my agents and the sacking of the safe house. He works for anyone who will pay him. The government kicked him out when apartheid ended he had too much blood on his hands. Fieldon is protected because of his connection to mining companies. It's too dangerous for you to stay here."

"I've worn out my welcome. I need to meet Erd can you arrange transport for me and the boy?" Jack said as he started packing his backpack.

"You are taking Theo with you?" asked Royce as he dialed his mobile phone.

"He is a good kid extremely sharp. He cannot go back to Zimbabwe. I will look after him until we sort this thing out." Jack responded.

"No problem, the airport will not work for transport. We have a plane at a private airport near Sun City about an hour and half-driving time from here. My driver will take you there. The pilot will be briefed on where to meet up with Erd. I hate to see you go Jack. I can use someone like you. We have a lot to do here. Go well my friend." Royce shook Jack's hand and hugged him and Theo.

A black sedan drove up to where they were standing. Theo climbed in and up into the back window to watch the city lights of Johannesburg disappear into the darkness. JB picked up Jack's signal. The phone JB gave Jack as a parting gift before he left for Zimbabwe rang.

Jack answered, "JB, that sophisticated hardware worked."

"We get lucky sometimes. You put on a big show in Zimbabwe. I assume that was your action we heard about last night. Right?" JB asked.

"It was not my party I just brought the punch. You need to know those folks had some of our toys. They had Sarin gas canisters from NATO and mj6 rockets made in the USA. The gas was supposed to be destroyed ten years ago. We have strangers in our house." Jack lowered his voice to a whisper.

JB responded, "That's what we suspect but without the one at the top we cannot move on them. Sarin gas is deadly stuff. Did you dispose of the gas after the party?"

"You think I would leave that stuff behind. You need to worry about who is slipping this stuff out of the back door. The canisters I saw came from the Germany NATO base. I recognized the seal from when I inspected the facilities there." Jack responded as he glanced out the back window of the car to check if they were being followed.

"Good work I will extend my retirement a few weeks longer to follow up on this lead. This may be what we need to turn on the lights to see where the rats run. By the way hope you are leaving Johannesburg soon we intercepted a call that put your head on a platter for two million rand." JB's voice turned serious.

"Retirement right, I must be getting better at this stuff. I'm popular." Jack tried to sound like he was not worried but the price on his head got his attention.

"Jack this is serious. This kind of money turns your friends into enemies. I could buy some good smoke with that kind of money. Watch your back.

Keep the lighter close it may come in handy." JB
voice cracking nervous he knew he could not help
him.

CHAPTER 23
BE FORMLESS

The old office was empty without any furniture. Simon had come to confirm everything had been moved. He reflected on the years he had spent making deals and learning his trade. Knowing it was time to lower his profile and focus on getting the business of the brotherhood well under the radar he'd decided to move his offices from New York to Newark New Jersey to a warehouse district near the port. Learning Maalik was missing and feared dead he had delayed the move too long. He remembered what Maalik told him, "Be formless."

Simon read the Art of War many years ago. He thought Sun Tzu teaching to be exceptionally insightful. He had forgotten about Tzu discussion on being formless to prevent your enemies from knowing how to attack you. Maalik was right the brotherhood needed to prevent enemies from undermining our mission.

He no longer conducted brotherhood business at the office. Instead, Simon used his nonprofit foundation to disguise his real activity of managing the finances of the brotherhood. Simon and Goode had formed the subcommittee that focused on acquiring the mining assets Maalik said would be needed to complete the plan to reshape Africa.

Goode filled up his passport with travel to Africa spending most of his time in Mali, Ghana and the Congo. Goode's legal training made him an excellent negotiator. He excelled at networking with government officials to obtain permission to acquire ownership of mining interests in Africa. Often Goode was mistaken for being from the Congo or Ghana.

Goode waited at the new office for Simon. He paced the floor in the conference room admiring several plaques honoring Simon for community work he sponsored since he retired. One that caught his attention was the Buford Johnson scholarship fund award for service. He observed that Simon really cherished this award because of where it was placed on the wall. Goode was standing in front of the plaque when Simon rushed in, saying, "I am sorry I'm late."

Goode responded, "No problem. I am admiring your wall here. Impressive, what is this one from the Buford organization?"

Simon walked over to the wall and got emotional. He said, "This one came from the town where I went to college. My best friend Buford started this scholarship fund with his estate after he died. His foundation awards scholarships to single mothers and children from broken families. I received this plaque from high school graduates who were the first to receive his scholarship. I volunteered to provide a week of career counseling for selected candidates. After they finished the students surprised me with this plaque. They used their own money to buy it to show how much they appreciated the time I contributed to help them prepare for college. The kids were all from Yale Street where Buford lived. Buford had changed my life. I went to see him after our first meeting at Rock Creek Park with Dr. Oble. Buford reminded me of what I had forgotten. In his own way, he showed me what was happening to our children with crime, drugs, and poverty."

"After my visit with Buford I started thinking of the ideas I had in college. We were going to change the world and help our people. I had forgotten this was still a part of me. He died before I could tell him how he changed my life. For me this plaque from the kids on Yale Street is my most cherished possession."

Goode said, "Brother, we are going to change the world. Let us get to this matter at hand. These are the final documents for the diamond mines in Ghana and Mali. Our company will take possession as soon as this agreement is executed and we transfer the funds to the escrow agent. Neither property has produced any minerals in the past five years. We received a favorable price. We need to finish this deal this week." Goode passed the documents over to Simon for signature.

"What is the urgency?" said Simon.

"I thought you knew. Jamal and Thomas found the treasure yesterday. Based on what we know now there are thousands of diamonds in the vault. There is a problem with how to remove the diamonds from the cave. I sent Brother Dawson, our engineer, to Honduras to work out a solution."

Simon said, "Did you say thousands of diamonds?"

"Yes, this is it. This is what Maalik and the old African told us to prepare for. Jamal thinks we are talking about more than a billion dollars in value," responded Goode.

"Billions? We need the mines to have a way to flow the diamonds into the market," Simon said.

Goode responded, "I've been thinking. Our objective should be to help African governments control the market for their own diamonds."

"Is that possible?" asked Simon.

Goode said, "I think so. We could collaborate with the Russians for diamond cutting and marketing. If we have a good quality product and we can secure the means to cut, it's possible. This quantity of diamonds will significantly influence the market for African diamonds. I identified several companies in Singapore, which are prime for acquisition that would give us the additional capacity. There are a lot if(s) and possibilities. However, first we need the stones to pull this off."

CHAPTER 24

THE SYNDICATE

The boardroom had not seen a meeting of the diamond men for at least two years. Order held the profits in check but now there were rumblings and complaints about security. Several mining concessions were lost to independent companies not aligned to the syndicate. Someone had to answer for what seemed to be cracks in control over the world diamond market. Lloyd Masters called an executive committee meeting of the governing board to take a measure of the situation.

Lloyd Masters ordered Eddington to attend and explain why he failed to deliver expected results. Masters did not care for Eddington. To Masters, he was the hired help. A commoner with no station other than what his family earned with blood on their hands. The Syndicate used men like Eddington to keep order and enforce their will with force.

Eddington diverted his plane from his trip to New York to attend the emergency meeting in London. The failed coup six months ago was the last straw. The syndicate financed the mercenaries who were arrested before the coup could be launched. Eddington was sure this would not go unnoticed.

The international investigation was getting close to the IBC. Several ex-military types from London were arrested with arms on the tarmac in Angola. Eddington assured Masters no one would talk. However the newspaper was filled with details of the failed mission with speculation other arrests were imminent.

There were no formalities to start the meeting. Masters gave the floor to Eddington for his report. Eddington skipped the production numbers instead, he started with the legend of hundreds of diamonds the size of eggs. He spoke of Jon Luc Eddington's life long search for a quantity of large diamonds stored away somewhere in Africa. Eddington told the committee if these stones ever surfaced, control of the world diamond market could be put in jeopardy. Prices would fall and the fortunes' locked in the syndicate's inventory of diamonds would disappear.

The room was silent for a few moments then Masters said, "Rubbish! This legend has floated around for over one hundred years in pubs and bars in every backwater-mining town in Africa. This is nothing but a yarn spread by fools. Why do you waste our time with this tale? What are you going to do to protect our mining concessions and keep the government out of our business?"

Eddington responded, "Our intelligence agency is working to cultivate a more cooperative political environment in three of the four problem countries shown on this chart. If you need details we need to talk off line. We are using contractors to persuade several elected officials that our syndicate offers the best prices and security for the mines and the product."

Masters pounded the table. He said, "We pay you for results. The dirty little details are for you to determine. Results are what we want."

The other board members joined in the chorus with pounding the table saying, "Results that's what we want."

When the room came back to order Eddington finished his cigarette and took the floor again, he said, "Rest assured you will have what you demand. Need I remind you of our track record over the last twenty years or have you forgotten how fat you've gotten with the profits as a result of IBC's assistance." Eddington lit another cigarette then said, "It's clear you have no interest in the diamond legend but mark my words if they exist this little club may become extinct." Eddington put out his signature powder blue cigarette on the floor and walked out of the meeting.

After the door closed behind him, Master said to the group, "That man is as distasteful as he is vile. Egg shaped diamonds, really! He is just like his father-chasing ghosts for treasure when the diamonds are in the ground in our mines. Let him continue his little egg hunt as long as they deliver the results we demand. This legend is of no concern to us." The meeting continued on to other agenda items.

Eddington was angry as he rode to the airport he called to check on the arms shipment headed for

West Africa and spoke with the agent in charge. He said, "Rambus, I am taking heat on our little problem. Are you on schedule with changing the guards at the presidential palace? We need to show we are getting results soon."

The voice on the phone said, "Our forces are on the border waiting for orders check the BBC in the morning and you will find a new leader of the popular front. Our troops will be marching on the capital by tea time."

Eddington replied, "Good keep an accurate account on the ammunition and weapons supplied when the new president is installed we want to be repaid with interest for our hardware. Make sure he understands the diamond mines are not negotiable." He hung up and boarded the plane for New York.

Eddington ignored Masters and the syndicate's comments about the legend of lost diamonds. He had doubts too but when the two large stones turned up in New York, the legend came to life for him and his father. They were out there. He could smell them. He knew he was close.

* * * * *

In New York, Rick Dodge met Eddington's plane. Rick was very familiar with Eddington. They had collaborated in the Congo in the 70's and later shared intelligence when Rick worked for the CIA. Eddington's position at IBC opened the door for Rick to leave the Agency to become a freelance contractor. The IBC became his largest client. Rick recruited other former agents and a few from a British Intelligence MI5 unit to join him to run small wars and assassinations in Africa. This in-person meeting was unusual as far as Rick was concerned. Rick asked, "Why did you want to meet in person?"

Eddington puffed cigarette smoke in Rick's face then said, "The phone is not suitable for this conversation. You need to put 100% of your assets to work on finding Thomas Jet and Jack Regis. It is worth $2 million to me. There is an extra million if you capture them alive enough to talk."

Rick said, "Jack is one of ours … not to mention these are US citizens you are talking about. My people will push back on this. Use your folks. This is too close to home."

Eddington lit another cigarette. He said, "Your failed mission in West Africa put me in a difficult situation. The missile strike in Cape Verde failed to produce any results. I am running out of patience. You are not hearing me. I am not asking. I know your secrets. My folks are on this but I need reliable information that only your people can provide. I need everything you got. I am sure you will do a good job for me."

Rick had no choice. Eddington flew to New York because he wanted Rick to see he was deadly serious. Eddington ordered the car to turn around to go back to the airport. Rick did not say anything else.

Eddington opened the car door turned to Rick, and asked, "How's your pretty wife? Don't you have two kids? The new school is just right for them. You need to keep them safe." He closed the door, climbed the steps to his plane, and smiled. Eddington looked up and said to the pilot, "It looks like rain. I love the rain don't you?"

Eddington had his own plans for the diamonds if he found them. *He would take over the market and put the syndicate out of business. He will show Masters and the rest of those blue bloods. Before he is through they will be begging to me to let them sell their diamonds in my market*, he thought. Eddington chuckled to himself thinking of Masters on his knees pleading for him to return his call would be worth it all. He hated working for people who had distain for him. For years Eddington took out their dirty laundry and cleaned up their mess without even a thank you from any of them. He thought, *I would show them the bottom of my boot when I find the treasure. I will ruin them all.*

He looked out the window of the plane as it flew passed the Statue of Liberty as the New York skyline faded in the distance. Eddington headed for the Cayman Islands to join the search for Thomas Jet. He was confident Rick Dodge would do the right thing.

CHATER 25
MILES TO GO

Rough water brought the fishing boat finally to rest in the harbor outside of the Puerto Cortes, Honduras. A tropical storm had rocked the travelers for twenty-four hours. Erd lingered below with seasickness for the duration. Jamal and Thomas stayed on the deck until they could take no more and retreated below. Jamal prepared a sketch of the cave and diagramed the bundles and baskets of diamonds. They were organized in rows by category for some purpose. He labeled the inventory by row in his notebook from the count he and Thomas completed. Thomas studied Jamal's sketch for hours. He thought, *What does this mean? Why did they organize the diamonds in this manner?*

He said to Jamal, "When we remove the diamonds we need to try to keep them in order to allow us an opportunity to figure out why they were configured like this."

Jamal said, "You are awfully optimistic. I cannot imagine how we are going to get this stuff out. Keeping them in order is the last thing on my mind."

"Look at your sketch the bundles and baskets are in alternating positions. In the cave I thought this was random but now it seems like this indicates a different type of diamonds in categories," insisted Thomas.

Jamal ignored Thomas' ramblings concerning the sketch. He studied the two diamonds they brought back from the cave. The blue diamond is the size of a golf ball. It is amazingly clear. His eyes were fixated on the brilliance of the stone. Jamal said, "This stone must be worth a lot of money?" The other diamond was stunning but the blue stone seemed to captivate Jamal. Erd was too sick to look at anything. She stayed out of sight until the boat docked.

Zek and two of the crew went ashore to re-supply. He returned with a passenger named Brother Dawson. Goode had sent Dawson to assist with solving the puzzle of how to extract the diamonds from the cave. Dawson, Jamal and Thomas being back together again was special for Thomas. He thought he would never feel connected again to the brothers.

Erd finally got back to her old self and took charge of the reunion. She reminded everyone for every minute that passed was an opportunity for the IBC to find them there and track them back to the treasure.

Dawson examined the stones and Jamal's sketch of the cave. He interviewed Thomas and Jamal to calculate the depth below the surface and the approximate distance underwater to get through the tunnel to the cave. Thomas brought back a sample of the material on the cave walls. Dawson studied the material and developed a computer model scenario to determine possible options. Dawson met with Zek to inventory the equipment available on the boat for the savage operation. After a few hours of analysis, Dawson came back with his findings.

Erd, Thomas, Jamal and Zek gathered in the galley for Dawson's assessment. First, he described the task of bringing thirty seven thousand diamonds of varying weight equal to a total of 29,000 ounces or approximately 1,800 pounds. He included the gold coins in his analysis but this was a minor footnote of his study. Dawson designed a process using a vacuum hose to suck the stones from the cave through the underground tunnel. He determined this to be the most discrete method of removing the stones and gold without attracting unwanted attention from local authorities.

"You mean like a vacuum cleaner hose?" asked Jamal.

Dawson responded, "Yes the pump suction will be robust enough to carry the weight and volume this distance. I have prepared a list of material we need to convert the equipment on board to recover the treasure."

"Do we need a larger boat? There is a lot of stuff down there in the cave," asked Jamal.

Dawson said, "If your sketch is accurate we should have plenty of room on board to store the treasure. We need to organize the material to consolidate the volume. This boat can handle four tons. We will have a little more than a ton if we include the gold."

Jamal responded, "You're the engineer." Erd dispatched Zek to go ashore to acquire the additional materials. The boat prepared to head back to Belize.

Thomas asked Dawson, "What about keeping the diamonds separated like they are organized in the cave?"

"Yes I considered this problem." Dawson handed Thomas a layout of the boat's forward storage room with a diagram of a series of bins overlaid for separation of the stones by the bundle or basket number.

"This will add time to the salvage operation but we can sack and tag each bundle when they are recovered and based on the sack number we can reconfigure the layout after we have all the stones safely recovered. If we worked a twenty four hour shift we could be finished in a day or two," said Dawson.

Luckily, for Erd the weather cleared. The sea was smooth for the return trip to Belize. The boat did not register again with the harbormaster. Instead, they went straight to work unrolling over three hundred feet of hose through an opening on the side port. Fishing nets were cast. The crew worked the nets to catch fish in case the local officials boarded them.

Jamal and Thomas headed back in the water to the cave with extra tanks. Dawson would stay below to monitor the pumps and measure the suction pressure. Dawson determined that volcanic rock on the walls would block the radio communication. He rigged up a wire line coupled to the hose to serve as a wired communication link to the cave.

Thomas remembered the entrance location to the tunnel under the reef. He and Jamal wrestled the suction hose and the extra tank through the tunnel. Thomas set up the communications unit and handed Jamal his earpiece. Dawson started the pump and gave the signal for a test run. Jamal operated the hose as Thomas poured out stones for the vacuum process.

Like magic, the diamonds disappeared into the hose and minutes later Dawson radioed, "We are in business. Let's rock and roll!"

After eight hours, one thousand pounds of diamonds were cataloged and stored on the boat. Erd and Zek sweated bagging and logging the stones based on Jamal's drawing. They are on schedule to complete the recovery on time.

The last to go through the hose were the gold coins. Dawson was concerned about the weight and size of the coins but all but one of the chests went through the vacuum. Thomas and Jamal would drag the last one through the tunnel to the boat.

The cave was empty now and only the Mali King's image on the wall remained. Thomas took several pictures of the king before and after the treasure was removed. Jamal finally got comfortable with the king's eyes following him around. In some way, the gaze of the old king comforted Jamal knowing the brotherhood would use the treasure to free Africa. They took one last look as they left the cave. Jamal shouted, "Look he is smiling at us, Thomas."

Thomas did not look back as he jumped in the water with the gold, and together they drug the last of the treasure out to the boat. Zek and Jamal went back to remove any signs of their expedition collecting the candy wrapper, trash and the empty bundles and baskets which held the diamonds. They left no evidence they had been there.

Erd knew that eventually others would find the cave; she did not want anyone to know the brotherhood got there first. After Zek boarded the boat, they pulled up anchor and headed to Cuba with fish and treasure. The diamonds were boxed and sealed as red fish. The rest of the catch was sold in Havana. Erd and Dawson made special arrangements for the red fish and paid the government extra duty for the use of the boat.

The red fish containers were loaded on the trucks with Dawson headed for Paris. Goode made arrangements for a warehouse and security for the precious cargo.

Erd, Thomas and Jamal boarded a Soviet era cargo plane an Antonov An-124 headed to Cape Verde. The plane was loaded with fifty-pound sacks of meal, sugar, and corn marked humanitarian aid from the world health organization. The flight was unscheduled. Its journey to Cape Verde with a stop in Canada went unnoticed by Rick in his search for the diamonds.

Erd breathed sigh of relief as the plane took off for their rendezvous with Jack and Theo. She was anxious to see the dagger, and the secrets contained within. Thomas grabbed his medallion and kissed it for good luck.

Safely in the air hundreds of miles from Cuba, Erd received a text message from Dawson. Erd read the message and turned to Thomas with a strange look in her eyes. She climbed over the cargo that separated her from Thomas and Jamal with her PDA in hand. She interrupted the conversation saying, "Remember the strange arrangement of the diamonds in the cave with diamond bundles and baskets with the odd positions for the gold baskets."

"Yes, it was perplexing. The diamonds were ordered in a random fashion but neatly lined up in rows. The blue diamonds were spaced in bundles in different locations in a matrix formation, but I could not figure out what it meant," responded Thomas.

At that moment, she held up her PDA to show an illustration of the diamond arrangement sent by Dawson. Jamal said, "It looks like a river with gold pockets along the banks."

Thomas said, "Yes, the blue diamonds might represent the river, and the gold baskets could be the location of gold along the river route."

They looked at each other, stunned at the possibility. They sat in silence while the drone of the plane's engine became louder. The weary passengers settled in for the long fight to Cape Verde.

CHAPTER 26
BOUNTY

Jack thought about JB's comment that the bounty on his head would turn friends into enemies. Before the car turned into the gate at the airport, he had the driver stop at a service station for a restroom break for Theo. Theo looked puzzled at Jack, indicating he did not need to go, but went anyway. Inside the store, Jack purchased snacks for their trip. He reached in his pocket for the lighter from JB and placed it in a bag of a waiting customer in line before him. He watched the lighter leave with the unsuspecting patron, thinking this was his insurance policy. He tossed the phone JB gave him in the trash as he walked out of the door.

Theo joined him at the car he grabbed Jack's bag and said, "I hope you got something better than beef jerky?"

Jack smiled and looked back at the lighter driving off in the other direction. He said, "Yes, there are some goodies."

The car turned on to a gravel road for the fifteen-minute ride to the hanger. They heard gunfire in the distance from the direction of the store. Jack said, "We need to hurry we have some unwanted company."

Fieldon's private commandos had gotten a tip that Jack was in the store. His men swarmed in from all directions killing the store clerks and two customers in the process. They searched the market with Jack's picture, but the dead bodies did not match his description.

Minutes later Fieldon received a call from Rick Dodge, "He's on the move three miles moving north." Rick tapped into JB's secure file and tagged the phone and lighter he thought maybe in Jack's possession. Fieldon dispatched a helicopter to chase down the vehicle with the coordinates provided by Rick.

With the second explosion, Jack thought, *There goes the lighter.* The driver pulled into the hanger to a waiting Cessna four-passenger plane. The pilot looking out to the east from where the explosions came motioned for Jack and Theo to hurry. He said, "It's getting hot around here they are getting close we need to get into the air."

Jack and Theo ran over and climbed into the plane. The pilot said, "You are cutting it close." The plane taxied on to the runway without lights and took off into the night.

Fieldon inspected the burned out car but the occupants did not match Jack's description. He called Rick back, "You guys have some bloody terrible intelligence. All I have are four dead bodies to show for my effort. Where is this guy, Regis?"

Rick said, "He must have been tipped you were coming."

"You just cost me a lot of money. Find him!" said Fieldon.

* * * * *

Rick located a leased yacht that had departed from Cayman Island around the time Thomas disappeared. CIA agents met the boat in Caracas, Venezuela where the boat docked for service. The agents searched the yacht and found fingerprints, which matched Thomas. They questioned the captain and crew. From the interviews, they compiled a description of the Cuban fishing boat Thomas and the others boarded four days before.

Rick used the coordinates provided by the captain and pieced together where the boat had taken them. He forwarded the data to Eddington on Cayman Island. Eddington personally led the search for Thomas. He chartered a boat in Belize to take him to the point off San Pedro. He went ashore and questioned anyone within a five-mile radius on land, but nothing turned up. The harbormaster for a price provided the records on the Cuban boat that registered days after they sighted the yacht in the area.

Eddington sensed he was close. He stared out to the cove at San Pedro and looked up at the sky. He thought, *Where would I hide treasure.* He peered into blue clear water and spotted something shining off the reflection of the sun. He ordered his assistant to retrieve the object. An hour later, he brought back a single gold coin. This is what Eddington needed. The next four days he had crews searching the reef looking for more gold but found nothing. Finally, one diver located hundreds of empty baskets on the sea floor.

Eddington started cursing at everyone he knew the treasure was gone. He called Rick Dodge, "Find them. They are here. They stole my treasure. I don't care what you have to do." His eyes were intense like a crazed man, sweat poured down his cheeks. He threatened Rick's life if he failed. Eddington said, "Your intelligence is old. I am always two steps behind them. Find them now!"

Rick said, "They took the fishing boat to Havana, Cuba. We have no assets there I will do what I can."

Eddington responded, "Not good enough. Do it find them. My men are following your family. Fail me and you will never see them again." He hung up the phone. Rick was getting desperate.

* * * * *

Jack's plane only had enough fuel to reach Cape Town. Theo marveled at the majestic flat-topped mountain overlooking the city. The pilot announced, "This is Table Mountain. It's quite a sight." Jack nodded as his mind drifted a million miles away.

Theo pointed at the cable car gracefully gliding up to the top wishing he would be lucky enough to ride. He knew this was impossible but he daydreamed anyway as the plane approached to land at the private airport.

Jack was aware it was not safe in Capetown. He thought the further away from Johannesburg the better until they could work out how to get out of the country alive. The two million rand bounty on Jack's head could entice someone in the government to turn him in.

Royce arranged passage on a container ship for Jack and Theo. The pilot provided Jack directions to the harbor. They would take a ferry to Robben Island and from there a small boat would take them to the container ship in the bay. He waved good-bye to the two warriors as Jack and Theo got in the taxi headed for the harbor.

The pilot readied his plane and took off before Fieldon's men could get to the airport. Jack tucked the mysterious dagger inside his shirt where he thought it would be safe.

Rick's CIA connections gave him access to all the toys and high-tech surveillance options. He had a Department of Defense (DOD) satellite track air travel out of the area where Fieldon conducted his search. The agency found only one plane had departed around the time Rick got the call from Fieldon that the car was a dead end. Rick requested the South African Security Agency (SASA) to track the plane. He forwarded the location of the airport in Cape Town where the plane landed.

Fieldon's Gulfstream G-5 was in the air headed to Cape Town when he got the call confirming the location of the airport where the plane landed. The G-5 was a perk from his security contract with a mining company. They never asked too many questions.

Jack had little time before they would figure out his location. He had done this himself tracking a target. Now he was the target.

Fieldon's men started checking the airport in Cape Town to determine if Jack had purchased a ticket. Fieldon's SASA contacts gave him access to airline information to help his search for Regis. Jack's taxi dropped him and Theo near the parliament building. Jack decided it is better to go to the harbor on foot to avoid an eager taxi driver alerting Fieldon's men of his destination.

Out of breath, Theo and Jack were finally on the Ferry headed to Robben Island. Theo was excited about seeing South Africa he felt like he was on vacation. Jack on the other hand was feeling like a deer in hunting season. Jack kept looking back toward the harbor to see if a boat was following them.

Theo was unfazed by the danger pointing back at Table Mountain enjoying the ferry ride. Finally, on the island Jack spotted the man described by the pilot who would be the contact for their passage on a container ship out of South Africa. The container ship would take them to Cape Verde.

As the small boat departed from Robben Island with Jack, Theo and their guide, the sound of an explosion could be heard in the distance. No one noticed but Jack. His heart pounded. He thought, *Friend or foe?*

The local news reported a crash of an airplane in Capetown near Table Mountain. All aboard were killed. Witnesses reported seeing a flash of light hit the private jet before it went down. Debris from the crash was visible on the forward approach to the mountain. Tourists on the cable car watched in horror as the plane crashed into the mountainside.

Government authorities suspected a surface to air missile was responsible for the tragic crash that killed Alexander Fieldon, four other men and the pilot. The official cause of the crash was reported as a mechanical failure. Fragments of a US made Stinger missile were recovered at the crash site. News of Fieldon's death reached Eddington in Belize. Eddington was angry to learn of Fieldon's untimely demise. He knew without him Jack would slip out of his reach.

Royce made a special trip to Capetown to get confirmation that Fieldon was actually dead. He lost two agents to Fieldon's thugs. Their deaths needed to be avenged. Eddington suspected the brotherhood was responsible for the crash but he would never know for sure.

A stranger approached Royce when he exited the airport; the man stopped him to ask the time. When he responded the man said, "Fieldon was a lot of trouble for us too. It is a pity his engine failed. If you talk to Jack let him know he still has a few friends."

The man walked away before Royce could ask any questions. He assumed the stranger was CIA.

* * * * *

Rick tracked communications in Cuba to isolate any unusual chatter concerning Thomas Jet or the fishing boat to Belize. Rick got lucky with an informant who gave up information about a shipment of Redfish being expressed shipped to Paris with extra security by military personnel. A description of Thomas was forwarded to Rick as confirmation. He confirmed Thomas's connection to the boat where the red fish was unloaded. Rick tracked the flight to DeGulle International Airport and alerted Eddington of the shipment. Eddington alerted his security director to trace the plane and make inquiries about the shipment of Redfish.

Eddington called ahead to have his plane ready to leave Belize for Paris. He was determined to supervise the search for the treasure. His palms began to sweat with anticipation of finding the diamonds. The eight-hour flight gave Eddington plenty of time to think about what he would do with his new fortune in diamonds. He contacted diamond cutters whom he had used in the past to alert them he would have an opportunity for their services. Eddington worked the phones until he fell asleep with the phone in his ear and a cigarette burning in his hand.

His phone rang and woke him up, "Sir, we have located the package. The containers of Redfish were off loaded and taken to a warehouse located twenty kilometers outside of the city. The truck that picked of the shipment did have some additional security."

Eddington responded, "Do nothing until I get on the ground. Pick me up at the hanger. Alert our friends in the government we need to gain access to the warehouse to recover some stolen goods. Pay them well. No one goes inside until I get there." Eddington terminated the call.

He thought about the last thing Maalik said to him before he died. Maalik was dying from punctures in his lungs. He was delirious fading in and out of consciousness.

Maalik said, "Ice diamonds, Ice diamonds…." Then he died.

Eddington had taken his souvenir for his ear collection but remained puzzled by what Maalik had meant by ice diamonds…until now. Eddington was convinced Maalik was the mastermind of the African treasure hunters. He had been tracking him for years. Now he would have his prize.

The black sedan arrived at the location where the redfish shipment was delivered. French police were already at the scene. The inspector in command waited with the Eddington's security director. He had his envelope filled with Euros neatly tucked in his pocket.

Eddington walked over to the two men. He asked, "Has anyone entered the building?"

The inspector quickly replied, "No sir, we have the area secured there is no one in the building. The security guard was told to pull back while we investigate."

Eddington smiled and responded, "Good job. Your supervisor will be complimented on your professionalism. I will need some time to inspect my goods." Eddington directed his security director to proceed inside and he followed closing and locking the door behind him.

The warehouse was an enormous cold storage facility with vaults lined with row after row of lockers. They inspected delivery logs for the shipment from Cuba of red fish. After about forty-five minutes, they found the locker. Eddington's heart started pounding faster, thinking of the power he would have with the diamonds in his control. He thought about rubbing the syndicate and Masters' nose in the dirt when his superior product takes over the world diamond market.

His face and neck turned red with the expectation of opening the crates to find the treasure for which three generations of his family had searched. When they opened the locker door Eddington became faint and stumbled back against a row of boxes.

He caught his breath and stood up. He said to his assistant, "Stay out here I want to open the crates myself."

The room was ice cold. Eddington thought this was what Maalik was talking about…keeping the diamonds on ice. He shivered as he moved the first crate to open. He cut the binding with his pocketknife and pulled back the package sheets.

He found fish. He delicately pulled out fish after fish thinking the diamonds were well hidden to evade customs. After looking through the first crate finding no diamonds, Eddington became frantic and dumped out the next crate on the floor. "No Diamonds!" He shouted. He dumped crate after crate on the floor until he had emptied all the containers. Fish were piled everywhere.

Eddington's face grew blood red, he was hyperventilating and distraught as he started rambling, "Where are they? Dodge said they would be here." He stumbled across the floor saying, "He's a dead man. Kill him….."

He sat with his head in his hands until his assistant said, "Mr. Eddington, we need to leave. The police are outside waiting. We should go."

Eddington looked up. He said, "Yes, yes you are right. We need to leave. Have our men clean this mess up. Yes we should go…" Eddington shuffled his feet toward the door then straightened up and headed to the car. He looked ten years older than when he went in the storage locker. His face was pale with no color and his eyes lifeless. The diamonds were gone forever and his warning to Masters would become true.

* * * * *

Rick Dodge rushed out of his office in a hurry after his call from Eddington. He had little time to gather his family to leave New York. He left his car in Brooklyn and took a taxi to the subway in hopes of buying time if Eddington's men were following him. On the train everyone seemed to be watching him. His mind started to play tricks with him.

Rick calmed himself enough to call his wife to confirm his children were safe with her. When he heard their voices, he thought his worst fears were unfounded. He relaxed and exited the subway. *His paranoia had gotten the best of him*, he thought.

Rick stopped to purchase a newspaper, as he turned to pay the clerk; a man bumped into him and embraced him as if he knew him. He whispered into Rick's ear, "The brotherhood will see you on the other side."

The stranger disappeared quickly melding into the traffic of hundreds of people on the subway platform. Rick was puzzled by the peculiar message. He looked down at his shoes and saw blood. He felt a warm sensation in his chest and there was blood on his shirt. Rick had been stabbed. The stranger's knife had cut several arteries near his heart. He had only a few moments more to live. Rick stumbled to the floor with his last breath, he said, "What is the brotherhood?"

Rick's murder surprised Eddington. Rick had been killed before he could exact his own revenge, Eddington became concerned. He thought, *Fieldon and Rick are dead. Am I next?* He shrugged off those thoughts then doubled his security at his fortress and now he waits.

Eddington opened a fresh pack of his designer cigarettes made especially for him by Lazard's tobacco shop in Paris. He chose a special tobacco blend from the Congo with light blue paper wrapping for his smokes. Eddington's father smoked this special brand, as did his grandfather. He would not smoke anything else. A courier once a week delivered a case of cigarettes to his compound in Brussels. Security was tightened now that Rick and Fieldon are dead. Even the cigarettes were inspected for tampering before being allowed to be distributed to Eddington.

After Maalik's death, Goode had taken a special interest in the Lazard tobacco shop. The little shop had no security other than a lock on the door that had most likely been there for over fifty years. The lock was easily compromised one evening and for the rest of the night Eddington's cigarettes were injected with a special additive. It was not a harsh tasting chemical; in fact, Eddington remarked this new batch had more flavor. The rich flavor was due to a slow acting poison compound. The chemist assured Goode death would come slowly and painfully at the end. There was no antidote, no cure just death within seventy-two hours.

Eddington was a dead man walking when he left the Paris cold storage facility. The symptoms had already started when he almost fainted in the storage locker. He thought he was feeling poorly due to the excitement of being so close to the diamonds but in reality, the deadly toxin had already started him on his path to join Rick and Fieldon.

His security director found his contorted body on the floor in his office. Glass from the jar that held the Eddington family trophies; the souvenir ears from over a century of torture was broken on the floor. These small pieces of humanity are now free from the Eddington clan, that began with Jon Luc finally ended with the death of the last-born Frederick.

* * * * *

Jack and Theo's ocean voyage ended at Sao Vicente, Cape Verde. Seasickness took a toll on Theo. He hoped this was his first and last time on a ship. Jack was relieved to be on dry land too, though he did not mind the open spaces of the sea. Royce arranged for someone to meet the weary travelers at the port and escort them to safety. The escort drove the travelers past the compound destroyed by a CIA drone attack months earlier. The guide pointed over to the rubble of the main building of the compound.

He said, "They almost caught us off guard. We evacuated two weeks before the missile strike. Security is tight."

The guide handed Jack and Theo blind folds for the remainder of their journey. After an hour's ride, the three men boarded a speedboat that bumped over rough water until finally arriving at the destination. Still blind folded the two men were searched again, then loaded into a jeep for the last leg of their trip. After Jack's adventure in Zimbabwe and South Africa, he did not complain about the security measures. Jack knew the less he knew the better. Theo was glad to be out of the small boat. He was scared but Jack steadied him. Jack patted Theo on the shoulder and described the steak dinner they would have at the end of their journey. The promise of a good meal was enough to distract the young man as they bounced along on the unpaved road.

Thomas and Erd waited in the canteen for Jack. Jamal and Zek had departed hours earlier en route to meet Goode in Ghana. The reunion would be special for Thomas, as he feared never seeing his old friend again. When Jack walked in, Erd hugged him then asked for the dagger. Erd disappeared into the maze of hallways in the underground bunker. Jack noticed that Thomas had changed. Thomas seemed taller than he remembered him, his eyes were dark and more intense, his voice deeper and his words were measured.

Thomas said, "My friend I am not the same man from a few months ago. This journey has taken me to the brink and back. Now, I know what my father meant for me to be. I know you have been on a journey too my friend. Funny we've come full circle."

Jack nodded and said, "Yes these last few weeks has been full of surprises. I'm still reflecting on what this means for the future. However, one thing is certain my life will never be the same."

Thomas said, "With Maalik gone the brotherhood needs a few good men to pick up the torch to continue the battle. I hope I can count on you."

Jack did not say anything. He just looked at Thomas and nodded.

* * * * *

Erd removed the dagger from the leather pouch and instantly warm sensations rushed over her body. While holding the object her mind flashed back to how she'd recovered the dagger six hundred years ago. Her ancestor died after successfully securing the dagger in the castle. Erd's heart raced as emotions filled her body. She sat frozen until the door opened.

Several men gathered around the table to view the sacred object. Erd caught her breath then proceeded to examine the dagger. The blade was made of solid gold with the handle constructed of Ivory. Diamond studs adorned the handle perimeter with two rubies embedded near the center with a huge emerald on each side. The priceless artifact was believed to have been used by the Zimbabwe king himself in ceremonies for members of his court to swear loyalty to him. The royal shaman was the keeper of the dagger. In the handle, he hid the last part of the prophecy preserved for over six hundred years unknown even to the king.

Three hours later the room grew restless because no one could find a way to open the handle of the dagger. Each man tried to find the secret key to unfasten the handle without destroying the dagger. Out of frustration, Erd slammed the handle against the table, causing one of the rubies to fall out. Inside the cavity from where the ruby had been mounted was a tiny latch. She released the latch and the handle opened.

The ancient script found inside was translated to read the following message: *Seek enlightenment through the green light.* Linguists attempted translations with several variations of the meaning of the script. They focused on the meaning of the green light and all eyes were on the emerald stones, over an inch in diameter. The green stones were striking, but revealed no secrets.

Erd and the others decided to start fresh in the morning to seek a solution to the puzzle. The words rattled in Erd's head all night. She woke up at 4 a.m. and went to Thomas' room. He staggered to the door to let her in. He was exhausted from travel and the events of the past few weeks but Erd was wide-awake. Soon she was screaming for joy bouncing up and down with Thomas against the wall. Thomas was sure everyone heard her. Erd did not care as she joyfully announced, "That's it. I know what they meant by the green light." She kissed Thomas and ran out the room with only his shirt to cover her nude body.

Alone in the conference room with the dagger Erd studied the emerald stones then pried out one from the handle. The stone is unusually clear with a prism on the inside edges. With a pin light, she attempted to determine if there was something engraved into the stone but found nothing.

Frustrated Erd gave up and laid the stone on its side in front of the pin light. She rubbed her eyes thinking about Thomas and returning to bed. On the wall behind her appeared a projection from the emerald through the flashlight beam. The image included a blurred script in the green light with diagrams. Unfortunately, Erd did not notice the images. The pin light batteries gave out before she turned around to see the secret message. She went back to bed disappointed.

The next day Jack and Thomas toured the underground facility. Their guide navigated over a mile of underground passageways through training areas and operation control rooms. Inside the maze was a hub of activity with monitors lined the wall with images of news networks and satellite feeds from remote locations on the African continent. Technicians huddled over computer screens monitoring communications of conflicts scattered over the continent.

Jack was amazed at the level of sophisticated technology amassed at the facility under the nose of European and Russian intelligence agencies, even the CIA. The lingering question in his mind was how an independent African intelligence agency could exist without the world knowing. *Impossible*, he thought.

* * * * *

In Newark, Simon was working on finalizing the documents left by Goode for the acquisition of diamond mines located in Ghana and Mali when the secretary buzzed his office. She said, "Sir, there is a delivery that requires your signature."

"Go ahead and sign for me," said Simon.

She responded, "I tried sir but he will only accept your personal signature, and you must bring your ID."

Simon was irritated that he had to go out to the warehouse himself to sign for a delivery. When he got there, the driver greeted Simon. He said, "Sorry Sir, but Mr. Goode paid extra to require only your signature for this delivery."

Simon said, "It's okay." He signed the log and watched as box after box was unloaded. After the last box was deposited, Simon closed the door and sent the staff home for the day.

He was puzzled as to why Goode would be insistent that only he sign for the delivery. Simon cut the seal on the top box and opened the lid.

Simon dropped his glasses and tears came to his eyes. He knew this was not the beginning of the battle to free Africa but now his new brotherhood was engaged in the fight.